THINK OF ME AND I'LL KNOW

THINK OF ME AND I'LL KNOW

Stories

ANTHONY VARALLO

TRIQUARTERLY BOOKS
NORTHWESTERN UNIVERSITY PRESS
EVANSTON, ILLINOIS

TriQuarterly Books
Northwestern University Press
Evanston, Illinois 60208-4210

This is a work of fiction. Characters, places, and events are the product of the
author's imagination or are used fictitiously and do not represent actual people,
places, or events.

Printed in the United States of America

10 9 8 7 6 5 4 3 2 1

Library of Congress Cataloging-in-Publication Data
Varallo, Anthony, 1970–
    Think of me and I'll know : stories / Anthony Varallo.
    p. cm.
    ISBN 978-0-8101-5240-3 (pbk. : alk. paper)
    I. Title.
PS3622.A725T46 2013
813.6—dc23

                                                    2013003995

♾ The paper used in this publication meets the minimum requirements of the
American National Standard for Information Sciences—Permanence of Paper for
Printed Library Materials, ANSI Z39.48-1984.

For Gus and Ruby

CONTENTS

ACKNOWLEDGMENTS

Alaska Quarterly Review: "After the Finale"

American Short Fiction: "Time Apart Together"

Cincinnati Review: "Some Other Life"

EPOCH: "Slow Car"

FiveChapters: "Tragic Little Me"

Hayden's Ferry Review: "No One at All"

Sou'wester: "Think of Me and I'll Know"

storySouth: "Lucky Us"

Sycamore Review: "Everybody Knew"

* * *

I'd like to thank the editors of the magazines where these stories first appeared, as well as Mike Levine, Sara Dreyfuss, Marianne Jankowski, Jane Bunker, and all the good people at Northwestern University Press for their editorial wisdom and guidance.

A special thanks to Christine Sneed for helping this collection find a home, and to Evelyn Somers and Terra Chalberg for reading early drafts of these stories.

I'm grateful to my students and colleagues at the College of Charleston, and to my wonderful family: my wife, Malinda McCollum, and our children, Gus and Ruby.

THINK OF ME AND I'LL KNOW

SOME OTHER LIFE

All day a little song loitered inside Mira's head, in part because it was sunny out, and the song suggested a summer day, but mostly because she was wearing headphones, listening to her iPod as she went about her work. It was her second week temping for an insurance company, but the song told her otherwise. It told her she was a netted butterfly pulsing toward the light. An ocean loosed upon a rocky shore. The insurance company was housed in a former elementary school; the offices were old classrooms divided into cubicles, conference rooms. Mira let the song fade, then took the headphones off and put the iPod inside her desk.

"The last girl never listened to music," a voice said, and Mira turned. A boy stood in the doorway, a kid. "So why do you?"

Mira closed the desk drawer. "I guess because I'm not her," she said.

The boy considered this. "She was the best one. She let me put all these papers into those drawers." He motioned toward a row of black file cabinets. "She was an actress," he added.

"Oh," Mira said.

"She gave me a nice pen once." His voice strayed to a smaller place. "And a poinsettia. For my sister."

Mira nodded. She did not, as a rule, love children. "Well, that was nice of her."

The boy shrugged. "I guess." He was about ten or eleven, Mira figured, but maybe older. He had blond, Cub Scout hair, and wore a red windbreaker that was too big in the shoulders. His eyes were small and wise; his lips masked a certain tension.

"This building used to be my school," he said.

"Oh."

"It was a good school. You got a scratch 'n' sniff for a B." He wandered over to a bulletin board crammed with notices, flyers, and office party pictures that Mira had already mocked in emails to her friends. "I cried when they closed it down." He reached for one of the photos and straightened it. "And Merilee still doesn't know."

"Merilee?"

"Merilee's my sister. We live across the street."

"Oh."

Mira glanced out the window. "That must have been weird, living so close to school," she offered. "Like on sick days. I'd be afraid the teacher would spy on me through the window."

The boy gave her an appreciative look. "Merilee would like you," he said.

At that moment Ted, the office manager, appeared from the back office. "Well, it's Robbie," he said.

"It is," Robbie said.

"And how is Merilee doing these days?"

Robbie shrugged.

"Still won't come over and say hello?"

"Can't," Robbie said, and Mira saw a change in his expression. He pulled a piece of paper from his jacket and folded it into quarters. "Here," he said, handing it to her. Up close, his skin was freckled and pale.

"Well, we'd all sure like to meet her one day," Ted said.

"We come over here at night sometimes," Robbie said. "You could meet her then."

"Sounds like a plan," Ted said. He gave Mira a look.

Robbie walked to the door and put both hands to the knob, pulling against its weight. "Merilee wouldn't like this door," he said, and then closed it behind him.

Mira unfolded the note.

Hello! it began, in a girl's neat, exuberant script. *Me again. Just wanted to say thank you for the beautiful poinsettia. I put it on top of my dresser. (Did you know that a cat could die if it eats a poinsettia? Don't worry—we don't have one anymore!)*

Next there was something crossed out, then the note continued:

Well, thanks again for thinking of me.

Best wishes and take care,

Merilee

P.S. Apple seeds are poisonous, too.

Mira handed the note to Ted.

"Oh Merilee," he said.

The year before, Mira had been engaged, but she'd broken it off. She couldn't say why, really, except that getting married seemed like a very good idea and then it seemed the opposite. She couldn't explain it. She wanted to explain it, but every time she tried to explain it she couldn't think of anything to say. Her fiancé said he understood. He wasn't angry; there was no point in being angry, he said, so he wouldn't be angry. He'd be there for her, for when she was ready—whenever that was. He wanted her to know that whatever she decided would be OK with him. It would. He wouldn't want her to think that he would feel one way or the other about whatever it was she decided, since he wanted the decision to be her decision and not something he'd accidentally influenced by letting her know how he felt about her decision, whatever it might be. She should think of him—if she thought about him at all, and he wasn't saying she should—as someone who only wanted the best for her, since wanting the best for her was all he ever wanted, and was, in fact, the thing that had led to them getting engaged, although he wasn't trying to say that he thought he was the best thing for her, necessarily. No. He was only saying that his wishes, in regard to her decision, were impartial, and should have no bearing on her decision, whatever it might be. The point was that he was there for her if she wanted him to be there for her; unless the idea of him being there for her was in any way depressing or imposing or wearying or cloying or anything like that. He wouldn't want it to be anything like that. That would be the last thing in the world he would want it to be. He looked up at her and offered a hopeful smile. "OK?" he said.

They were sitting in a café. They were always sitting in a café. Mira had unwisely ordered hot chocolate; she usually finished hot chocolate in about thirteen seconds flat. She sucked on chocolate foam and nodded at her fiancé. What she wanted him to say was, "Don't be dumb; let's just get married."

"OK," she said.

He took her hand in his. "But it's OK if it isn't," he said.

One Thursday afternoon Mira took a break from imagining she was outside and went outside for a break. There was a playground next to the parking lot, fitted out with a tall swing set, sliding board, jungle gym, and a row of sea horses on rusty springs that nodded in the breeze. Mira went over to the swing set and sat down on the middle seat. There was a puddle her feet would need to pass, so she raised them, toes out, and began.

One pass. And a truth. Her life was going nowhere.

Second pass. But what feeling in her legs. And the clouds above.

Third. She could quit. Trees were so good.

Fourth. Every human enterprise was an attempt to approximate the beauty of a tree.

Fifth. She couldn't quit. Not for a while, at least.

Sixth. One of the sea horses was waving at her.

Mira braked and tried to disguise the surprise in her voice. "I thought you were a sea horse," she said.

Robbie's look was serious. "Only little kids rode the sea horses. And girls. The boys got the swings." He gave the sea horse a little kick, sending it juddering like a smacked antenna. "Merilee likes this sea horse. She wanted to come over and ride it last night, but I said it was too cold."

"You guys really come over here at night?"

"Sometimes. We can't come over in the daytime." He put his hands in his pockets and toed at the dirt beneath the sea horse. "Because of Merilee."

"You know, I hate to tell you this," Mira said, already sensing that she would later wish she had been more kind, "but a lot of people around here think that Merilee doesn't really exist." She watched Robbie describe a circle in the dirt. "I'm not saying I don't, but—"

"But you do," Robbie said. "You believe." He approached the swing set and stood before her. "I told her all about you. I told her what you said about the teacher spying through the window. She really likes you."

Why? Mira wanted to say, but instead studied herself in the puddle, an elongated blob with crisp, perfect shoes. She looked up now, and saw Robbie watching her with new curiosity. "Why can't Merilee come over in the daytime?" she asked.

"She can't go out in the sun. Not for more than a few minutes. Or else." He made a sizzling noise and grabbed at his arms.

"She has some kind of disease or something?"

Robbie nodded. "No sun."

"How does she go to school then?"

"She doesn't. Me and my mom teach her everything. Plus we get these videos in the mail. They're totally cool. Did you know that Beethoven used to keep his pee under his piano?"

"Robbie," Mira said, searching. "Do you see why all of this might be a little hard for someone to believe?"

"No."

"You don't?"

"No. Why shouldn't they? It's no lie."

"It's just that—" Mira began, but a change in Robbie's expression blocked its passage and opened another, where a girl and her brother sat side by side on a long white sofa, watching television with thick curtains drawn tight. "I'd like to meet her," Mira said.

"Her, too," Robbie said. He put his hands in his pockets and regarded the building with one eye closed. "You can see in at night. Through the blinds. I keep telling Merilee not to look, but it's getting harder and harder." He kicked a stone a remarkable distance. "One night she's going to find out it's not a school anymore."

"She doesn't know?"

Robbie shook his head.

"How could she not know?"

"Merilee listens to me," Robbie said.

"What does she think about the company sign?" Mira said.

"I told her that was a project."

"A project?'

"Uh-huh. Like the time capsule," Robbie said. "Did you know there's a time capsule by the old cafeteria stairs? There's a toothbrush in there. Plus a yo-yo."

There were shadows from the trees that Mira had not noticed until now. For a moment they offered up something wise and obvious to her, but what? Robbie walked over and sat down on a swing, twisting lazily from side to side.

"Everything in my life is something I don't want to do," Mira said. "I don't want to go to work; I don't want to go home. I don't want to say 'good morning' or 'good night.' I don't want to watch TV; I don't want to turn it off." She looked over at Robbie. "Do you know what I mean?"

"Nope," Robbie said. Then he stood and said good-bye, leaving Mira to the shadows and the day stretched dauntingly before her.

At the temp agency, Mira's interviewer had asked her what quality she most admired in a boss.

"Translucence," she'd said, chancing a joke.

To her surprise, they placed her anyway.

Part of Mira's job was to sort and deliver the mail, which she didn't mind. She liked steering the mail cart through places where people weren't, through the copy room with its ghost scent of fresh milk and damp mittens, past the women's restroom, where the afternoon sun sometimes revealed blond lettering G I R L S etched into the dark-stained door, and beyond the collections office, where the occasion of turning the doorknob always left the vaguest feeling of chalk dust between her fingers.

Mira entered the office now, pushing the door open with the cart. She saw an employee sitting on a computer chair in the center aisle, his back to her. He was wearing dress pants, dress shoes, and a crisp white undershirt. Two other employees crouched next to him, laughing. Other people peered over the tops of cubicle dividers, watching whatever was going on. Mira's first thought was to turn around, but one of the employees—the guy with the Pez dispenser collection—addressed her and she froze.

"Don't mind us. We're just gluing pennies on Francis."

The room rang with laughter.

Mira felt her face grow hot, and tried to smile. "Oh," she said.

She made her way to Francis, who sat grimly in his chair, as one woman dabbed his undershirt with glue and the other pressed pennies into place. "Do you want me to leave these on your desk?" Mira asked, indicating the letters.

"Bitte," Francis said. "Wunderbar."

Mira nodded, and one of the women turned. "Do you want to do one?" she asked, holding out a penny.

"No," Mira said, "that's OK."

"Sure?"

"Yeah."

"All the cool kids are doing it," the woman said.

"I know, but—sorry."

"All the hipsters," Francis said.

Mira felt tears form in her eyes. "Sorry," she said. "I'm lame."

"That's OK," the woman said. "We'll get you next time."

"Yeah," Francis said. "All the cool kids want you in the scene."

Mira nodded and felt as if she'd just lowered herself into a hole. "Sorry," she said. "I really am. Sorry."

In the bathroom, Mira checked herself in the mirror and reviewed everything she'd done wrong. This took a while. Then she dampened her hair and took a drink from the faucet. The water was warm and unpleasant, but it presented a truth nonetheless: stop saying sorry so much. Mira wiped her mouth and pushed through the bathroom door, awakened, renewed—and immediately knocked into a woman carrying a potted geranium.

"Sorry," Mira said.

The woman knelt and scooped a line of dirt back into the pot. "Oh, that's OK," she said. "He's been through worse."

Mira knelt down to help, but the woman told her not to worry. "Hey," she said, putting her hand on Mira's shoulder. "No use crying over spilled . . . dirt."

Mira shook her head. "Sorry."

Mira walked back to her desk without the least recollection of doing so. Outside, sunlight bloomed against the windows, coaxing the color out of the panes and placing it about the room. Brightness was where brightness usually wasn't. Mira noted the difference, and then another: a note on her desk.

Dear Mira, the note began.

How are you? (don't you hate letters that start that way?) I thought I'd tell you my favorite thing and see if it's your favorite thing, too. My favorite thing is when you've got guests coming over and you've just put out the biggest bowl of potato chips and just as the doorbell rings you take the potato chip that is at the very top of the bowl and stick it in your mouth. That's my favorite thing. (Besides Altoids—do you like them?)

Just wondering.

Merilee

"He gets his mother to write them," Ted had told her, the day Robbie handed over the note. Together, they'd watched him hop the playground fence, stopping to free his windbreaker from a snag. "She's some kind of weirdo. Came over here one time and told us to stop parking in her driveway. Well, there wasn't anyone parking her driveway. There wasn't a single car in her driveway. Not one. So I said, 'No one over here is parking in your driveway, but I'll let everybody know, just in case.' But she said that wasn't good enough. She'd been blocked in all morning. Couldn't get here, couldn't get there; well, she went on and on. So I said, 'Let's go have a look and I'll see what I can do,' and we went outside and of course there were no cars in her driveway, so I said, 'Looks all clear to me,' and she said, 'They must have just left.' Crazy lady," Ted said. "I feel bad for the kid."

The homes across the parking lot were partially eclipsed by the rise of a sharp hill, and by the tall, flowered weeds that Mira sometimes watched with a certain fascination, seeing things she could not possibly see moving within, like tiny hands and manes of hair. They were town houses, connected in twos, with short lawns between them, and gravel fronts with cars parked under ports. A few had back decks with screened-in porches, others without, and one unit—the last in the row—had a bedroom window with plywood boarded across the panes.

Once, on her way to meet her ex-fiancé for dinner, Mira slowed into the drive and cut the engine. She sat for a moment, considering what she would say if someone opened the front door, when someone opened the front door. A woman stood at the door, older, her hair whirled inside a bath towel. She looked at Mira as if she were a felled oak.

Mira rolled her window down. "Sorry," she said.

"Are you?" the woman said. She had one hand on the doorknob, the other propped against the jamb. "Why?"

"I must have the wrong house."

"The wrong house. What's wrong about it?" The woman gave Mira a look she wasn't sure how to read.

"Well, sorry again." Mira started the engine. "Thanks anyway."

"If you say so," the woman said.

At dinner, Mira's ex-fiancé talked excitedly about downloading music from the local library, a new interest of his, as was fishing, something he used to do as a kid but hadn't done since. He was also really getting into cooking eggs. It was amazing how good baked eggs tasted, something he'd forgotten about. Bacon—that's the secret to everything. You can't beat bacon. Remember bacon? He was finding all these old things he'd forgotten he liked, he explained.

"Take this shirt," he said, and opened his sport coat to show her the dress shirt he was wearing, cornflower-blue with a wide collar. "I must have bought this thing before I left for college, but I swear I've never worn it, not once. Just something I'd forgotten about. And now I'm wearing this shirt like two times a week. Three. It's ridiculous. It's like my favorite shirt ever."

"That's good," Mira said.

"And radio. I'm listening to the radio all the time now."

"Radio?"

"In the car. On the way to work, at home—I forgot I could listen to the radio at home. Who listens to the radio at home?"

"Nobody much," Mira said.

"Exactly. But try it out sometime and you'll be like, 'Wow, how cool is it that I'm in my house listening to the radio?' " He made the face he sometimes made when he was really thinking about something—Mira had forgotten about that face. "There's something really comforting about it. Like you're even more *inside* your house than you'd normally be. Does that sound stupid?"

"No," Mira said. "I think I get it."

"Try it sometime and see," he said.

"OK."

Later, they went to a bar and had no fun whatsoever. A band was playing classic rock covers, the lead guitarist studying his fingerings like they were puzzles to solve. The lead singer clutched a spiral notebook. The drummer kept adjusting the height of his cymbals. There were only a few other patrons in the bar, four women sitting at tables near the stage, watching the show with rapt inattention. When the band took a break, the women handed the band members water bottles and orange wedges. Face towels. Handi Wipes. A Subway sandwich.

"My God," Mira said, "it's their *mothers.*"

Her ex-fiancé gave her a questioning look.

"The band," Mira explained. "They're kids."

A week after receiving the note from Merilee, Mira worked her last day at the office. They threw her a going-away party, gave her a card signed by people she'd barely met, made jokes about the freedom of being a temp. *Congrats on getting out of here!* someone had written. *School's out for summer!* Mira told everyone thanks, ate a second piece of cake so sweet her teeth ached. She'd been offered the job there, a permanent, part-time position, but Mira had turned it down.

"I need something full time," she'd said. "Sorry."

"Hey, we understand," Ted said. "We're sorry to see you go."

Really? Mira wanted to say, but didn't.

Her temp agency placed her with an advertising company, a "fun, crazy bunch," her placement representative had told her. And they were, stopping by the reception desk so often Mira had to feign reading email to keep them at bay. Clever college grads full of irony and Red Bull. She liked them well enough, though, liked being in the middle of the sea of worries that rose whenever a deadline neared, everyone storming past her desk with dry-erase boards and laptops, her boss once screaming, for the entire office to hear, "All I'm seeing here is cream cheese, people! It's not the cream cheese; it's the emotion *behind* the cream cheese!" Mira got invited to parties she neglected to attend. She went out for drinks once or twice, sipping lime gimlets while her coworkers tried to draw her into conversation, kind coworkers, although Mira was always relieved to return to her car and pull her seat belt across her chest. She ate her lunch outside, and hung her coat on the back of her chair. She did not correct the UPS guy when he called her "Maura," as her squiggly signature mistakenly confirmed. She kept no coffee mug atop the agency microwave.

And she was only a week into her new position when she called things off with her ex-fiancé. He said he understood, except for how he didn't, really. Why had they spent so much time deciding? he wanted to know. She had to admit, it seemed strange to have spent so much time deciding when she ended up deciding the same thing she'd already decided. Mira couldn't answer, since the truth was she'd never been deciding—she'd made her decision way back when she'd broken off the engagement. But she hadn't really known that. Or she did, but she didn't want to. It was hard to explain.

"It's hard to explain," she said.

They were sitting in her apartment, which seemed suddenly too small to Mira. Her ex-fiancé was wearing a new sweater. It was late. They'd been to a movie neither of them wanted to see, but they couldn't think of anything else to do, anywhere else to go. What is the appropriate date for an ongoing broken engagement? The movie wasn't funny, but Mira couldn't tell if it was supposed to be or not. It was the kind of movie they normally might have enjoyed making fun of, afterward, if they weren't in the middle of breaking up again. They would have enjoyed making fun of it together. But they didn't. They sat in Mira's too-small apartment and didn't say anything. They sat there for a long time. Mira's ex-fiancé kept rubbing his hands together, the way he sometimes did when he felt anxious. Mira was glad she wouldn't have to deal with him doing that anymore—it had always bothered her more than she liked to admit—but then she felt guilty for feeling glad so she put her head to his shoulder, which was uncomfortable. Outside, it began to rain.

"Look at the trees," Mira said. She could see them through the window, their branches turning in the wind.

"Yeah," her ex-fiancé said.

"Big storm," Mira said. "Yikes."

"Do you think you could give me the engagement ring back?" her ex-fiancé asked. "I hate to ask, but."

"No, I understand."

"It's a little lame."

"No it isn't."

He shrugged. "A little bit it is."

But when Mira tried to take the ring off, it wouldn't budge. "Hold on a minute," Mira said, and went to the kitchen sink, ran her hand underneath the water. "Is it hot or cold that makes it come off?"

"Hot, I think."

But the hot water didn't do anything. Cold made the ring tighten its grip. Mira rubbed dishwashing soap between her fingers. The ring spun loosely in place, but would not slip past her knuckle. "It's not working," she said. "I don't know what to do."

"What about butter?" her ex-fiancé said.

"I've got olive oil," Mira said, but the bottle only contained a teaspoon's worth, which made her fingers glisten, but did nothing to release the ring. "Jesus Christ," Mira said. "This is so embarrassing." She could feel herself beginning to cry.

"Don't worry about it," her ex-fiancé said. "It's no big deal."

"It's horrible," Mira said.

"You can just give it back to me whenever it comes off."

And that's exactly what Mira did, one week later when she was watching TV and idly turning the ring with her fingers, not really even thinking about it; it just came free. She held the ring in her palm, recalling its once familiar weight. It had been a nice ring. Mira sealed it inside a bubble envelope and placed the envelope inside her purse. When she left the envelope in his mailbox, she couldn't decide whether or not to put the little red flag up. She sat in her car, the window rolled down, her ex-fiancé's house dark—he worked nights; she wouldn't run into him. It occurred to Mira, sitting there deciding whether or not to put the flag up, that she really wanted to keep the ring after all. But she placed the envelope in the mailbox anyway.

When the advertising agency offered Mira a full-time position, she had already started dating David, a copywriter, although they weren't letting anyone in the office know. It was a secret, like Mira's recent broken engagement, which she hadn't quite gotten around to telling David about. Not yet. She would, she knew, in time. David was a few years older than Mira, had been married and divorced, and had one child, a girl, Judy, whom Mira had met only once, at an agency barbeque, Judy falling into step with the other children her age, throwing sticks into a pond, and chasing a yellow dog around the yard. Mira had sat with David and a few other coworkers, not saying anything, the fact of their relationship silently ballooning from her head like a cartoon thought: *don't you see us sitting so close together?* Later, after Mira had returned to her apartment, David had called her and asked if he could come over. Could he? He felt bad about today, he said, not doing more to introduce her to everyone, especially Judy. God, he felt terrible about that. Was she angry with him?

"No," Mira said.

"And I can come over?"

"You can."

He did. He knocked. She answered. He'd brought her a bottle of local ginger ale. "I don't know why I brought you this," he said. "But here it is."

"Thanks," Mira said, "it's perfect."

"Except for how it isn't," David said.

She poured the ginger ale into two tall glasses. They drank the ginger ale and talked. She told him about her engagement. He told her about his marriage, the divorce, the challenges of raising Judy—and the pleasures, too, because he didn't want to be one of those parents who was always talking about how difficult it was to be a parent. It really wasn't, not all of the time at least. "I'm slowly being replaced by a series of interactive videos," he joked. "Judy is disappointed that Daddy doesn't come with a Vivaldi soundtrack. Plus my Spanish is for shit."

Mira told him she was afraid she never "came across" around other people—that's how she'd always thought of it, anyway. She told about her previous temp jobs, hiding out in her cubicle, eating lunch outside, away from everyone else. How she timed her arrival so that she wouldn't bump into anyone in the parking lot. The time she accidentally locked herself in the bathroom, but couldn't bring herself to call out to the janitor just outside the door. Breaking the door open with the weight of her body.

"You can run away now if you want to," Mira said.

"Offer declined," David said.

He told her so many things and she, in turn, told him so many things, that he couldn't notice, even after she'd mentioned a strange little kid who used to visit her at work, that there was a hole in her story, something left out. For Mira told him about Robbie and the playground and the notes from a mysterious little girl everyone knew was actually the boy's crazy mother, feeding Robbie's fantasy of a sister who came out at night and peered into windows, thinking a defunct school was still a school. Mira did not tell David about pulling up in the driveway and talking to the woman in the towel. She did not tell him about keeping Merilee's notes in her nightstand drawer, where she sometimes took them out before falling asleep, the notes opened and closed so many times their creases had begun to wear thin. Up close, the notes exuded the smell of strawberry lip gloss and fabric softener.

For a secret to be a secret, it must be one forever. And that is why, even as Mira grew closer to David and felt her heart going out to him—she really could feel this, a pleasant departure—she did not tell him about the nights she drove to the old school and parked in the parking lot. How she went there night after night, waiting. The school's floodlights were on, casting bright halos across the playground. She could see the swing set and the sea horses, the sandbox bereft of sand. She could see the window where her office used to be, home now to some other temp, some other life. Her breath fogged the windshield; she wiped it away.

And then she saw them. Two kids entering the floodlight's circle. A boy in a familiar windbreaker and a girl bundled into a winter coat, although it was not cold out. If they regarded Mira at all, they made no indication of it. They started on the swings; Mira could hear them talking, heard the swings creaking. When she stood from the car, she saw them turn and look at her, this boy and girl, out too late, ducking the sun. For a moment, Mira expected them to run. But they didn't. The boy waved and shouted something to her. The girl let her swing come to a stop. And Mira could just make out the girl's face as she walked closer and heard what the boy was shouting.

"We forgot your name," he said, "but we knew you'd come."

TIME APART TOGETHER

If you remember Great Bank America at all, you probably remember them from their billboards, especially the one of a teacher standing in front of a classroom of children, the chalkboard transforming into a credit card when you drove by—remember that? The way your eye would register the scene for a moment, a smiling teacher with her hand raised to the board, and then, voilà, a Great Bank America Visa Gold Card gleaming like a freshly minted coin? It really was sort of impressive, the way everything about Great Bank America was back then, in the glorious nineties, when they employed nearly twenty thousand employees—people, Great Bank would say, *people*—including me. I was twenty-one, a college dropout, and the oldest member of a high school punk band called Death to Popularity. We had been together for two years but had written only eight songs, all of them exactly the same tempo and length, with remarkably similar lyrics and chord progressions, and titles like "Backstabber" and "Stabbed in the Back," which we swore, at drunken postpractice parties in suburban garages, were completely different songs.

I had a girlfriend then, too, Ursula, although I often pretended like we weren't together. We'd met when I was in school working at one of the campus dining halls, hosing off grimy trays or serving lasagna so burned on the bottom you had to pry it free with a butter knife. I noticed Ursula coming in a few times before she started talking to me, a gloomy sophomore with a pixie haircut, unlaced Chucks, and a Celtic tattoo across her left shoulder. She had a habit of taking an apple from the fruit bowl no one ever touched and rubbing it with her shirt, then tossing it back into the bowl. As other people moved away from my station, Ursula would stay, taking forever to decide between ziti with marinara sauce or spinach linguine.

"There meat in that?" she'd ask, pointing to the marinara sauce.

"It's marinara sauce," I said.

"Doesn't look like it."

"That's what the sign says."

Ursula gave a disapproving laugh. "The sign," she said.

But what she did more than anything was stare at me. Really stare, in a way that made me feel embarrassed and uncomfortable—there was no flattery in it. Sometimes I'd catch Ursula out of the corner of my eye staring at me from the soft-drink fountain, where she stood with another friend—Kathryn, I'd later learn—who dressed just like Ursula, and who nodded enthusiastically at whatever it was Ursula was saying. When I met Ursula's eyes, she quickly looked away.

One day Ursula came to my station and placed a photograph in front of me. I was covering someone else's shift, hungry and hungover, and was contemplating a way to make dropping out of college seem like an inspired move, a career change, a promotion. *Well done,* I always imagined someone saying about me dropping out, although it was never clear who was saying this or what I'd done well. *Well done.*

"You're not Kevin," Ursula said.

"I'm Brad," I said.

"That's me and Kevin at the beach," Ursula said, and I picked up the photograph to see a picture of Ursula and me standing in front of a crackling bonfire. Ursula had her arms around me; I clutched a Corona in one hand and was giving the photographer the finger with the other. Same haircut, same smile, same height and build—even, I noticed, the same tendency to tilt our heads slightly to the right in photographs.

"He looks just like me," I said.

"Everyone says so," Ursula confirmed.

"He was your boyfriend?" I asked, but Ursula grabbed the photo and placed it inside her book bag, which was freckled with band pins, all the obvious stuff: Minor Threat, Operation Ivy, The Misfits. The same bag that I'd later see in my apartment, morning after morning, after we got together, where Ursula kept a change of clothes, her cigarettes, her notebooks, and a starter's pistol the approximate size of a cassette tape.

"Why do you carry that thing around?" I asked, the morning after we'd first hooked up. It was early, but not early enough that my roommate wouldn't need to be back soon to get a shower before classes began. Ursula pulled a T-shirt over her head.

"Kevin gave it to me," she said.

"Your boyfriend gave you a starter's pistol?" I said.

Ursula changed her bra underneath her shirt—it always sort of impressed me how quickly she could do that—and shrugged.

"Kevin always liked me having it," she said. "He used to carry it around in high school, to keep people from jumping him. People were always starting things up with Kevin. Like, one time he was walking through his neighborhood and this white van just pulls up out of nowhere and three guys get out and beat Kevin with a Wiffle ball bat." Ursula shook a cigarette from her pack and flicked her lighter open. "Another time he was driving late at night and a car full of football players tailed him for miles, shouting at him through a megaphone, *Pull the vehicle over, pull the vehicle over!*"

"They had a megaphone?"

"So Kevin started keeping this in his glove compartment." Ursula held the pistol and regarded it warily, one eye closed. "Not a bad thing," Ursula said, "to have around."

"Let me see," I said.

The pistol was as smooth and gray as a soda can's interior. The barrel was tipped with plastic, a joke, a clown's weapon. I raised the pistol to the ceiling and pulled the trigger. The trigger didn't budge.

"And they're off!" Ursula said.

My parents separated the year I started dating Ursula, although their separation began with them moving to different parts of our house and speaking in whispers whenever I visited, which wasn't often. I had never been really close to my parents, but my first two years away at school seemed to have made them both strangers to me—or maybe it had always been that way, and I only needed some distance to see it. In the months leading up to his departure, my father started chopping down trees on our property, old maples and elms and poplars, trees it turned out I had great feeling for, although it took my father's chain saw to help me understand that. I'd visited my parents only twice that year, but each time our property grew barer and barer, the grass along the driveway choked with sawdust. Branches lay in heaps atop our woodpile, their ends wearing dead leaves.

"Why is Dad chopping down trees?" I asked.

My mother laughed. "Because that's what men of a certain age do," she said. She was folding clothes for me to take back to my dorm.

"They chop down trees?"

"He's out there nearly every night," my mother said. "Chopping and sawing. Won't wear safety glasses. Won't pay someone else to do it for him. Such a handyman."

"Maybe you could tell him to stop," I said.

A few moments later, my father came in from the garage, where he now went to retrieve beers from the tiny red cooler we used to take with us to the beach. He'd set up our old couch and coffee table in the garage, too, plus his ancient stereo and LPs. Sometimes I'd hang out with him there and sip beer and listen to records without either of us saying a word. He'd strung Christmas lights across the ceiling, a blinking sky of strange constellations.

"Hi, Bradley," he said.

"Hi, Dad."

"School treating you OK?"

"Yeah."

"Good. That's good." Then, "You look good."

"Thanks."

"Hope you'll stay for dinner."

"OK. Maybe."

"Stop chopping down our trees!" my mother said. She looked at me for support. Her expression was one I would come to know well in the months that followed, a mix of anger and resignation verging on tears. I looked back to my dad, but he only disappeared back into the garage. Later I found him hauling old tires out to the curb.

I dropped out of college a few months after I started dating Ursula. I didn't think of it as dropping out, though; I thought of it as time away. Time for me to move into a cheap apartment and get a part-time job at Great America Bank. Time for band practice twice a week, with Ursula in tow, the two of us stopping off at a liquor store to buy Colt 45 and Night Train for the other band members, seventeen and thankful, who paid me back with cash they'd stolen from their parents. Time to feel bad about dating Ursula, whom I had little feeling for and who often invoked Kevin's name as if Kevin were someone watching over us, some departed spirit, some disapproving seer, as in "Kevin would never park this close to a mailbox," or "Kevin would never order fried calamari," or "Kevin always liked the way I looked in these overalls," when Kevin was wherever Kevin was, not that I cared, really. Time for me to think about the four incompletes I'd taken, courses I told myself I would eventually complete, without quite believing it, courses like Professor Thompson's Shakespeare seminar.

I was supposed to write a twenty-five-page paper about the fool in Shakespeare's comedies, but I couldn't get past my initial thesis, which was that the fool proved *the impossibility of love*—a phrase I'd stuck in the opening paragraph for no more reason than the sound of it—and ended up asking for extension after extension, meeting Professor Thompson in his basement office, whose lone window looked out onto the library parking lot, and from behind whose door classical music always blared, requiring me to knock until my knuckles ached.

"The impossibility of love," Professor Thompson said, reading my first page as I sat across from him, his reading glasses perched atop his head, his expression somewhere between mild concern and benign amusement. "What does that mean exactly?"

"Well, that's kind of the problem," I said. "I'm not really sure."

"The impossibility of love," Professor Thompson repeated. He had a faint British accent, which everyone said was an affectation, as was his occasional habit of glancing out the classroom window for minutes at a time, until someone would ask "Professor? Professor?" before Thompson would return to his lecture as if no time had passed at all.

"The impossibility of love," he said. "Seems to me one of those phrases that means whatever the person employing the phrase happens to think it means."

"Hm," I said.

Professor Thompson laughed. "Like 'self-esteem' or 'holistic education.'"

"That's interesting," I said, which is what I always ending up saying whenever I met with Professor Thompson. That, or "I see."

Professor Thompson read to the second page, and then began flipping through my paper as if it were a magazine. He stopped every now and then to read a sentence aloud, but didn't say whether this was because the sentence was good or bad. After a while, he put my paper on his desk, facedown. "It never ceases to amaze me," he said, "the lengths a student will go to make everything fit his or her argument." He gave a little laugh. "By hook or by crook."

This seemed a fair assessment of nearly every paper I'd ever written. "I never believe a thing I'm saying," I said. "When I'm writing a paper. Not one word. The whole time I'm typing, I'm thinking, What a bunch of lies."

Professor Thompson looked at me with a wry smile. "The truth is what we make it," he said.

"I see."

Professor Thompson turned his chair so that he was partially looking out the window. "May I ask you something?" he said.

"Of course," I said. "Sure."

"I don't mean to offend you, but I feel like I can ask you and you'll answer honestly: why did you choose to come here for college?"

"I don't really know," I said. "It's cheap, I guess."

"It is that," Professor Thompson agreed.

"And a lot of my friends were going here," I said, which was true, but it was also true that those friendships had faded away by the end of freshman year. "I guess I couldn't really think of anyplace else to go."

Professor Thompson nodded. After a while, he said, "Thank you. For being honest. It's something I've always wanted to ask my students, since I started teaching here. Why would anyone go here? The campus is crowded, the library third-rate, the town ugly, and the students seem to regard their studies as a kind of afterthought, or at least many of them do—the ones who trudge into my classroom at least." He laughed. "Could be I'm the problem, eh?"

"No," I said. "Everyone knows this is kind of a party school."

"A party school?"

"Yeah," I said. "You never heard that?"

"They neglected to mention it," Professor Thompson said, "during my interview."

"Oh," I said, then glimpsed Professor Thompson's smile. "That's funny."

"What does that mean, a party school?" he asked.

"Well, you know," I said, "like everyone here just likes to get wasted and blow off classes and hang out and whatever. My freshman roommate had a .8 GPA," I said, which was true, although I didn't mention that we used to get stoned together, smoking pot through a pipe made out of a fabric-softener box. Mr. Nice, we used to call that pipe.

Professor Thompson shook his head. "A party school," he said.

"It's the kind of phrase that means whatever you think it means," I said, and Professor Thompson laughed as heartily as anyone I've ever heard since.

"Thompson is such an ass," Ursula said, when I told her about our meeting. "Fucker gave me a C-minus in Renaissance Tragedy." We were sitting in my dorm after a morning of sex and near-breakup talk, a conversation I kept trying to put into play, but Ursula kept kicking out of bounds. (Me: You know, I'm really falling behind in my classes. Ursula: That's why I'm here to help you. Me: But I really think we need some time apart. Ursula: We can spend time apart together.)

"I don't know," I said. "I kind of like him."

"Thompson? Are you serious?" Ursula exhaled a cloud of cigarette smoke.

I recalled Professor Thompson's expression as he stared out his office window. "I think he understands things," I said.

"Fake British fucker," Ursula snorted. "Even Kevin couldn't stand the guy."

My job at Great Bank America was to call people in the middle of dinner and trick them into transferring their credit-card balance from a competing bank to their new Great Bank America card. I wore a headset as I did this. I sipped weak coffee and spun a little blue-and-gold tassel someone had unwisely tied to their cubicle chair. I addressed people as "Ma'am" or "Sir." I said things that I never said outside of work, like "let me tell you something honestly" or "that's where we come in" or "we like to give folks options" or "that's the GBA difference" or "sounds like a plan." During breaks, I sat in a too-brightly lit cafeteria and made fun of the people I'd just spoken to. I made fun of the woman who shouted, "Diane Sawyer told us about you!" and the man who made me sing "Hail to the Redskins" on speakerphone, or the umpteen million callers whom I'd put on hold while I pretended to take their names off the phone solicitation list. I made fun of the phone solicitation list. I made fun of Phil, a coworker who wore his headset during break, and who read the sales script with the grim intonation of a hostage testimonial, and who often sat across from me at break, making fun of me for making fun of him. We made fun of our manager, Steve, for his ponytail and paisley ties, for his square-toed shoes and faith in firm handshakes and pep talks, which he made while massaging our shoulders in a way also worthy of making fun of, whispering things like "eye of the tiger" or "only the strong" as we lured people deep in debt into even darker waters. We made fun of ourselves. We're the kind of people we'd hang up on, too, we agreed. We would! Take us off the phone solicitation list—or else!

But the thing was, I secretly enjoyed my job. I was good at it, in a way I wasn't good at almost anything else, like being a college student, drummer, dutiful son, thoughtful boyfriend, or finisher of Shakespeare papers. I liked arriving early to work and going through the night's leads, a cheap tie loose from my collar, but a tie nonetheless. I liked preparing to do a job well. I liked the sound of my voice when I said, "Hi, this is Bradley with a quick courtesy call from Great Bank America. Sorry if I'm calling at a bad time." I liked the way I could often subdue the most resistant customer by adopting an attitude of nonchalance—appear too eager and you're dead, *dead*—about the pitch, as if I, too, had some doubts—sure, who wouldn't, my tone seemed to say—but I was willing to put those doubts aside if you were, too. What's that? You are? Good, that's good. I think you've made the right choice. I really do. You know what? I'm happy for you. Congratulations!

Sometimes, after an evening of work, I drove to band practice. We tried to practice our eight songs, but we were never able to play any of them all the way through. We'd stop a few measures in, when the bass player forgot the bridge, or the singer couldn't hear where he was in the chorus, or I realized I was playing a different song than the guitarist, who pressed the latest pedal his parents had purchased for him and stared out at me from within a haze of sonic whatever. "Stop, stop, stop," our singer said, waving his hands. "OK, that's enough. We'll figure it out next time." But we never figured it out the next time. We'd practice again a week later and fail to play any of our songs all the way through. We forgot our eighth song entirely, whatever it was, something about greed. Greed was in there some-where. Our singer checked and double-checked his spiral notebook, from which he sang lyrics none of us had ever actually heard.

We practiced in our bass player's garage, our girlfriends seated on sports lockers and patio chairs, sipping wine coolers and malt liquor while we played half a song, stopped, played the next half of a song, and argued whether we'd actually played our seventh song already—had we? We asked our girlfriends; our girlfriends weren't sure. Maybe we had, maybe we hadn't. Why don't you just play it again?

Ursula came to some practices. She'd sit on a workbench she'd place behind my drum set, watching me from behind. I always hated when she did that, the feeling of her looking over my shoulder as I tried to remember whether this was the part where I rode the high hat in open eighths, or beat out fat quarter notes on the tom-toms, Ursula's cigarette smoke invariably drifting over me at the exact mo-ment I recalled that this was the part where the drums didn't play anything at all, a moment of rest before I was supposed to do a quick fill on the snare. If I dropped a stick, Ursula would immediately hand me one over my shoulder, even though I kept extras atop my bass drum and had told Ursula countless times I didn't need her to hand them to me.

"Of course you do," she'd say. "Who else is going to help you?"

"Please stop helping me," I said. "I don't need you to."

We were driving back to my terrible apartment where I knew I'd apologize for treating her like such a jerk, which would beget other apologies for all the times I treated her like a jerk, which would lead to me saying how sorry I was, which would lead to sex, which would lead to me staying up later than I intended and barely making it to work on time, where my lies lost a little off their fastball.

"You need me for everything," Ursula said.

I laughed. "Isn't that a little desperate?"

Ursula began to cry. "You're such an ass," she said.

All the more to break up with me, my dear, I thought. "I'm sorry," I said. "I shouldn't have said that."

Ursula didn't say anything.

"Come on, don't be mad," I said, wishing to rip my voice from my throat and toss it out the window. "I said sorry."

We were pulling up behind a minivan where two kids stared blankly from the back windows. One of them wore a wolf mask beneath a white football helmet. "Look at this kid," I said.

Ursula stared out the passenger's side window.

"You should see this kid," I said.

But Ursula only dragged her finger along the windowpane, drawing something I would never know what.

When my parents finally separated, my dad moved into our beach house. I only visited him there once, and brought Ursula there another time when I knew he was away, Ursula and I having sex in the guest bedroom where, as a kid, I'd always been afraid a wave was going to drag our house to sea, although the ocean was several blocks away. It was the off-season, most of the shops along the main beach drive closed for business, the old arcade I'd wasted so many childhood hours in now a Popeyes chicken, open, but empty. The saltwater taffy shops dimly caged within their security gates. The ocean brown, bereft of skim boards.

"Kevin's family has a place down here, too," Ursula said.

"Great," I said. "We should go visit."

Ursula gave me a look that intended to say how poor an idea that seemed. "Kevin wouldn't like that," she said. "Kevin hates surprises. More than anything in the world. That's something he always made me promise him, that I wouldn't surprise him. Ever." Ursula smiled.

"Good man, that Kevin," I said. "Straight shooter."

"He would always say, 'Surprise me and I just might surprise you back.'"

"Surprise me and I just might surprise you back? Doesn't that sound a little bit insane?" I said. "Like something a guy stroking a Persian cat in front of a computerized map of the world might say?"

"Don't be stupid," Ursula said. "Kevin hates cats."

Although the beach was essentially closed, our band had somehow managed to get a gig at the lone vegan restaurant in town, where I set up my kit in front of a window festooned with flyers for yoga classes, tai chi, indie film festivals. That night we played our eight terrible songs, stopping in the middle of each to figure out where we were, somehow making it to the end, dazzled and amazed we'd finished. A funny thing kept happening to me that night: somewhere in the middle of each song I started thinking about my Shakespeare paper for no real reason that I can remember. The restaurant was empty, save for two employees in headscarves and an inexplicable family of six seated at a table along the back wall, whose collective indifference bore no resemblance to the thematically resonant blabberings of Feste, Puck, and Dromio, but there they were, wanting my attention, it seemed, as I muted cymbal crashes with my bare hands and lost two sticks in the course of one song. *The impossibility of love.* Or was it the *possibility* of love? Had my thesis really been inside out this whole time, tonight seemed to ask, and I was the last one to know it? A drumstick appeared in the corner of my vision.

"Take it!" Ursula shouted.

I turned to look at her. She was holding a drumstick and looking at me like I was no one she knew.

"Why won't you leave me?" I asked, too quiet to hear.

Ursula reached out and struck my ride cymbal in time with the downbeat.

A few months before everything ended with Ursula, I interviewed for a managerial position at Great Bank America. I didn't want the job, but my manager insisted I go for it. "You'll be lights out," he said. "You just get in there and show them what we've been seeing around here, OK? You're one heck of a salesman."

Am I? I wondered, and felt a mix of dread and pride.

As I was about to leave his office, my manager looked me over and said, "And listen, when you go in there, you might want to wear a white shirt, OK?"

I looked down at my shirt: a blue dress shirt with a buttoned collar. Dry cleaned the day before, light starch. "Why a white shirt?"

"Well," my manager said, "because a blue shirt kind of asks the question, 'Why not a white shirt?'" He gave me a look that intended to be sympathetic. "Know what I mean?"

Unfortunately, I did. I knew exactly what he meant. Perfectly. And that's why I knew I'd wear a white shirt and speak in sales-speak and give a firm handshake and make the kind of impression that had lured so many people into switching their accounts to Great Bank America. I'd get the job. I knew I would. I'd get more money, get a better apartment maybe, probably quit the band. I'd dump Ursula, too, of course, that was without question. She'd cry, of course, and I'd feel terrible and tell her how sorry I was, but secretly I'd be glad to move on, maybe even hook up with a co-worker who'd been hanging out with me during breaks lately and who kept promising to come to one of my gigs, and who had given me enough signals to understand that I could think of her as she thought of me, our feelings as obvious as the cigarette smoke that drifted between us during breaks. Ursula would call me out on all of my shitty behavior, all of it microscopically observed and remembered ("you forgot it was my twenty-first birthday until the bouncer said something," "you pretended to have mono when I asked you to meet my parents," "you act all cold toward me when I'm having my period," "you made me stand outside in the snow for twenty-five minutes so you could watch an overtime football game and then lied about not being able to hear the intercom," and "you've never told me you loved me, ever, even when I say it to you, and always say 'what do you want me to say?' whenever I've pointed it out it to you," and "all of my friends think you're a complete asshole; even Kathryn, and Kathryn likes everyone—everyone!"). I knew that this last one, the weakest of the bunch, really, would be the one that would push my buttons since I cared more about what other people thought about me than what Ursula thought, and I'd end up agreeing with her, and those agreements, one building upon another, would lead to us getting back together, our relationship cemented, as it was, on the joint understanding that I was a complete asshole unworthy of Ursula's interest in me. I couldn't agree more! We have so much in common! We wouldn't break up at all; we'd keep seeing each other. I'd take Ursula to the Great Bank America holiday parties, where everyone would ask us when we were going to get engaged. I'd sip eggnog and fantasize about dumping Ursula, while Ursula squeezed my arm through the fabric of the first suit I'd ever bought in my entire life.

And maybe that's why I showed up for my interview fifteen minutes late, sans shower and shave, wearing a purple shirt I'd worn only once before for a cousin's wedding, from which I'd strung a holiday tie patterned with Donald Duck and Goofy skiing endlessly into each other, their expressions preternaturally joyful, oblivious to their fate. Donald had neglected ski goggles; Goofy's tongue wagged dangerously from his slackened jaw.

"Bradley?" the manager said, extending his hand. His office was adorned with golf memorabilia.

"As in Milton," I said.

"Milton?"

"Milton Bradley," I said. "The game guys."

"Oh, right, right," the manager said. "You had me there for a second."

"Connect Four. The vertical checkers game from Milton Bradley," I intoned.

"Ah, right."

"Pretty sneaky, sis!"

"Right," the manager said. "Well, why don't we have a seat and you tell me a little bit about yourself?"

I did. I took a seat (Me: This is a really comfortable chair. Manager: Thank you. Me: No, I'm serious. This is like, the most comfortable chair I've ever sat in, ever. Manager: Glad you like it. Me: How can I like it, when I *love* it? Manager: . . .) and told him a little bit about myself. I told him how I liked the way my voice sounded when I talked on the phone (Manager: That's crucial to customers), how I enjoyed the feeling of making a sale (Manager: Good, good), especially when I'd formed some kind of personal connection to the customer (Manager: That's so important, isn't it?) and knew the customer thought I was exactly the kind of person I wasn't (Manager: I'm not sure I . . .) and carried with them an idea of me that was totally false (Manager: Well, we're not promoting false . . .) and was absolutely and completely and totally the opposite of the person I really was.

"And who is that?" the manager asked. He'd already closed the folder in which my résumé now darkly dwelled. His screen saver showed a hypermagnified golf ball upon a hypermagnified tee.

"What was the question?" I asked.

"The person you really are," the manager said.

"Hey!" I said. "I just remembered your name. It's Lionel."

"It is," Lionel said. "Listen, Bradley—"

"That's a name you really don't hear much anymore, do you?" I said. "And it's such a cool name. *Lionel.* Wow! Why aren't there more Lionels in the world?"

Lionel gave me a pitying smile and extended his hand. "I think I'll tell Jim we had a nice talk, but maybe this isn't a position that's right for you." His handshake was loose.

"I was going to say I had no idea," I said. "The person I really am."

To my surprise, I didn't lose my old job. I kept showing up to work with my shirt tucked in, my hair not quite dry, my sales numbers good, great even, another day of lawful lies done right. I did take Ursula to the company holiday party, but it wasn't as a new manager at Great Bank America; it was just me the Customer Advocate and the girlfriend I couldn't shake, no matter how many times I stared blankly at her after she told me she loved me, or how many tearful arguments we had after every pathetic band practice, Ursula thrusting drumstick after drumstick into my empty hand. (Me: Stop it with the stick thing, OK? Just stop, stop, stop it! Ursula: You never say thanks for anything. Me: Stop the stick thing and I'll say thanks. Ursula: You know what? The more you do for someone, the more they act like an asshole. Me: Right! So do less! Do less!) We stood together in a lobby fitted out with ice sculptures and chocolate fountains, from which bartenders wearing elf hats poured me five too many chocolate martinis, a drink I despised, but kept ordering again and again, for no reason other than to get chocolaty drunk, while avoiding talking to Ursula, who'd worn a little black dress to the event, and who looked pretty good in it, and whom I knew I'd end up having highly regretted sex with later that night, the dress catching beneath the bedroom door when, the next morning, I closed it behind me and got dressed for work in the bathroom.

But I was wrong. We didn't have highly regretted sex. Instead we got into a fight on the way home. I don't even remember what started it, except that it was snowing and Ursula was driving and some combination of the snow and martinis gave me the sudden license to break up with Ursula forever. World without end, amen. I said things that made Ursula cry, things I'd normally apologize for, but didn't. I said more things that made Ursula cry on top of the ones I'd already said. I kept going. Ursula called me an asshole. I was the biggest asshole that ever was.

"So what does that make *you*," I said, "for being in love with the biggest asshole that ever was?"

Ursula pulled the car over. We were somewhere near my old campus. A painterly moon sent pale light across an unpainterly parking lot. Behind the lot, a forest whose bare branches surely must have acquired snow, as did my dress shoes, a few moments later when I stepped from Ursula's car.

"Get out," Ursula said. The car was stopped along the side of the road.

"What?"

"Get out," Ursula said. "I never want to see you again."

"You're breaking up with me?" I said. "Wow, that's funny. That's the funniest thing I've ever heard." I began to laugh. I laughed heartily, meanly, lustily, with no remorse and not a little joy. I couldn't stop laughing. Not until Ursula said, "We were never really together," and drove away and left me in the snow, because she was right and I was drunk and cold and standing in the snow and the nighttime is darker than you think it is.

I ended up hitching a ride with a guy named Donnie. Donnie liked to party, he said; Donnie was always up for a party. Donnie Party, some people called him, they did. Did I know about any parties? I looked like the kind of guy who knew about a lot of parties. I told Donnie I didn't know about any parties, and had him drop me off at the campus from which I dropped out months ago—the only place I could imagine letting Donnie drive me to.

ANTHONY VARALLO

"You give Donnie a shout if you hear about any parties, OK?"
Donnie said.

"I'll let Donnie know," I said.

"Deal," Donnie said.

I'd already figured out how I could catch a bus from campus, but
I ended up wandering the quad anyway, not really wanting to go
back to my crappy apartment, not yet. My fingers had warmed up
enough in Danny's Camaro, and it was sort of nice to be walking
through the quad with the snow falling and my new independence
from Ursula draping me like a gift scarf. I found myself walking
toward the English department, although I hadn't planned on going
there, the department a brick Georgian wannabe whose lights were
out, save one, one low window still inexplicably bright, its window
shades likewise inexplicably drawn on the most inexplicable office of
them all, Professor Thompson's. Why had Professor Thompson left
his office lights on?

I approached the window and peered inside. I saw Professor
Thompson's desk, stacked with student papers, all of them likely as
vacant and shapeless and undercooked as my own. The radio boom
box which countered Professor Thompson's daily dismay with Mozart
and Haydn. His desk chair, gray and ink-stained and pushing twenty,
its wheels cracked. I saw these items as a part of my past, displaced by
a present that had somehow left me behind (my paper, once in the
stack, was now presumably gone, tossed away). And even though I
recognized these feelings for the self-pity they so horribly were, my
recognition didn't stop me from picking up a traffic cone (why was
there a traffic cone near the English department? There was!) and
hurling it toward Professor Thompson's window. It made a sound
I've never forgotten since, a sustained sudden thrumming, which
I felt in my knees. The traffic cone fell to the ground. The window
didn't break. Even so, I ran away as if it had.

The last show I ever played with my terrible band was at the beach, again, in the same vegan restaurant whose flyers still hadn't changed. We had learned our eight songs by then, had even added three others, and had made a promo tape that got a little radio play at local college stations. Not much, really, but enough attention that we sometimes had a decent crowd for our shows, high school kids with backpacks and zines to sell, bored college kids getting drunk between sets, sucking down warm beers in the alley behind the restaurant, where I hung out, too, drinking, talking to the guys in my band or the few women who sometimes paid me mild interest. I'd drink two beers in a matter of minutes, listen to a band equally terrible as ours, then do the same thing after the next set.

Our set went OK, except I kept dropping my sticks. I don't know why, really. It's not that hard to hold onto the sticks, but it's also true that once you start dropping them you can't stop, your hands refusing to dry, slick with sweat. I remember looking out in the crowd, which was fitted out with a few kids who must have known the words to some of our songs, singing along in a few places, an idea that depressed me. And I must have been scanning the crowd more than usual because I saw Ursula standing at the back of the restaurant, watching me. I tried looking away, but it was no use. She moved to the front of the crowd, where a few stupid kids were ironically slam dancing. One of them was wearing a red ski cap even though it wasn't cold out, and the cap must have had a large pom-pom on top that shook as he danced, because I remember thinking it was funny the way the pom-pom was shaking in time to the song and where had Ursula gotten to when Ursula materialized beside me and held the starter's pistol to my head.

"Bang," Ursula said, or something like that, but I'll never know.

"Ursula?" I think I said, and, at that moment, a boy in a hooded sweatshirt jumped from the crowd and knocked the starter's pistol out of Ursula's hand. The pistol fell to wherever the pistol fell. The song stopped. The boy placed his arms around Ursula as if to restrain her, but she didn't need restraining. She put her arms around him

37

and held him tight, her shoulders shaking, her head buried in his black hoodie. The boy stroked her hair as if she were a kid waking from a nightmare, and spoke soothing things into her ear. They sat that way for a while, the two of them locked in some kind of trance until I crouched beside them and chased the trance away.

"Kevin," I said. "It's you."

Kevin looked up at me, his face mine, his expression mine, the look I sometimes turned on Ursula when she told me she loved me, me wanting her gone. There was something Kevin's look wanted to reveal to me, but it wasn't until Kevin reached out and pulled my shirt from its buttons and placed the first of his many punches against my temple that I understood what it was.

"Kevin!" Ursula was screaming. "Kevin, don't!"

And I felt Kevin's blows against my head and tasted blood on my teeth and finally grasped, at long last, the impossible possibility of love.

EVERYBODY KNEW

The day of his class presentation, Jacob came to school dressed in grocery bags. He'd fashioned a jacket and pants out of paper sacks, the pants belted with plastic bags; the buckle he'd cut out of box tops, the box tops glued together, sturdy as a new comb. It was Jacob's intention to wear this outfit as he delivered a speech about the environmental repercussions of paper and plastic grocery bags, an idea that came to him over the weekend when he'd been tasked with throwing away all the grocery bags his mother had been storing beneath the kitchen sink. Jacob had carried the bags to the garage when the bags seemed suddenly beautiful to him—they really did, the way they collapsed into themselves like paper fans, their faint inner perfume—and he saw it all at once: him, standing before his amazed classmates, whose collective hilarity would need to be quelled by Mrs. Scheer before he could begin his speech, which would end, after bursts of spontaneous applause, with him donning a canvas grocery sack, whose side his mother would permit him to gouge with eye holes, and declaring, "Saving the earth—it's *in the bag!*"

But, on the morning he was to deliver his presentation, Jacob first had to go to a dental appointment.

"The dentist? Why did you schedule me for a Monday morning?" Jacob said. "I'll be late for school."

"It was all I could get," his mother said. She was driving him to the appointment in the station wagon Jacob would inherit as soon as his learner's permit yielded his driver's license. The station wagon had a Ducks Unlimited bumper sticker Jacob planned on scraping off with a razor blade the moment he got his license. Sometimes, for no real reason, Jacob found himself thinking about scraping off the Ducks Unlimited bumper sticker with a razor blade. He was sixteen years old.

"Don't tell me you're upset about being a little late to school," his mother said.

But Jacob didn't say anything. If he soaked the bumper sticker with soapy water, it'd peel off like nothing at all.

They sat in the waiting room for what seemed like hours, Jacob's mother watching the *Today* show while Jacob flipped through *Sports Illustrated.* "Boy, when they say come in at quarter of eight, they really mean eight twenty-six, don't they?" his mother said.

"If they don't call me in the next two minutes, we're leaving," Jacob announced.

"He said," his mother said, "as if it were up to him."

To Jacob's mounting anger, they called him in a moment later, and promptly fitted him out with a heavy bib and a suction tube that curved into his mouth like a strange lure. The tube made embarrassing wheezing noises and kept slipping down onto his tongue. Jacob stared at a ceiling freckled with smiley face stickers. When the hygienist finally came to relieve him of his humiliation, Jacob had come to a realization about his speech: it would be cooler to say, *Environmental destruction? Just bag it!* instead of the thing about saving the earth. He could even raise his hands, touchdown-like, for added comic effect.

When he arrived at the school it was already after ten o'clock.

Mrs. Scheer's class would already be in full swing, everyone wondering where he was, an F looming for his persuasive speech grade, 30 percent of his final score. Jacob changed into his bag outfit in the passenger's seat, while his mother straightened the sleeves. Running across the parking lot, it occurred to Jacob that the outfit was remarkably comfortable and well designed, maybe the finest thing he'd ever made, something his sort-of girlfriend, Zoe, would be proud of—she had once made a T-shirt out of men's cotton briefs but was too embarrassed to wear it in public. Jacob had been grateful for that.

Jacob stopped at the principal's office to get a late slip. The receptionist looked at his outfit with what should have been amusement, Jacob thought, but instead handed him a hall pass without comment. Her eyes seemed raw from tears, or maybe Jacob had never really noticed them before? The other receptionist—the one who usually came from lurking in the back to offer a peppermint candy from a wicker basket—stayed at her desk, locked into a solemn phone conversation, the receiver cradled to her turned head. Down the hallway to Mrs. Scheer's class, Jacob's outfit made a noise like hastily raked leaves.

When Jacob opened the classroom door, Buddy Hamilton was in the middle of a presentation about legalizing pot. Mrs. Scheer had forbidden this topic, but she sat at the back of the room with a tolerant expression, her eyes meeting Jacob's at the same moment the rest of the class turned and spotted him in his grocery bag outfit. Jacob quickly took a seat near the front of the room, unusual for him, king of the back row, where he and Zoe launched incredibly biting observations from behind tented notebooks, their fronts inked with band logos. Buddy looked at him for a moment, a look that passed quickly but left behind a whiff of contempt nonetheless. Was Buddy Hamilton giving him dirty looks? Buddy returned to his spiel, which was studded with comic opportunities Buddy passed by as if they weren't even there, delivering his argument as colorlessly as if he were reciting the Pledge of Allegiance. Jacob chanced a look at Zoe, but couldn't quite glimpse her from where he sat.

"Thank you, Buddy," Mrs. Scheer said, amid a smattering of weak applause. "Very informative."

Buddy nodded and sat down without giving his usual peace out sign. By now, a few classmates were whispering about Jacob's outfit, or so it seemed to Jacob, who felt his face begin to warm. He could hear Mark Gaudry saying something to Mike Hartlett, something mean, most likely, but that was Mark Gaudry, Jacob reasoned, who had always had it in for him, ever since the time freshman year when he'd taken his place on the debate team and led the team to a fourth place finish in state quarterfinals. Well, let the Mark Gaudrys and Mike Hartletts conspire against him; he had this crowd otherwise. Why else would Mrs. Scheer sometimes allow him to run the vocabulary workshops, Jacob walking the room with Mrs. Scheer's coffee mug in hand, a pretty lame gag overall, but one that had been captured in last year's yearbook, with the caption *Mugging it up again, Jacob?!* The hardest secret for Jacob to keep was how good he was at subduing a hostile audience. Of course he'd never say so, but the fact was that he had a way with people; they couldn't resist his humility, his willingness to risk embarrassment, his disregard for being cool, his staunch, unapologetic pose of no pose whatsoever. His raging likability.

"Jacob," he heard Mrs. Scheer say. "You're next."

Jacob gathered his notes into one hand, the canvas grocery bag in the other, and crinkled to the podium. The podium rocked when he placed his hands upon it, but Jacob knew better than to grip its sides, a rookie error. His speech began, as all good speeches do, with an example: "It's Friday evening. Raining. You need to pick up something quick for dinner. Maybe stop by the supermarket on the way home. Push your cart through the aisles—hey, why do you always pick the cart with one stuck wheel? Or does every shopping cart everywhere in the world have one stuck wheel and you're the last person on earth to know it?" He looked up from his notes to see if anyone was laughing, but put away his smile when he saw Zoe's expression, blank as Susan Kennon's and Amanda Gervon's, whose faces radiated embarrassment nonetheless. Jacob returned to his notes, but not before registering a few quiet sobs. How had he lost this crowd so quickly?

Jacob redoubled his focus. Stick to your notes. Hit your marks. Enunciate, enunciate, enunciate—why couldn't anyone seem to understand that enunciation was three-fourths of the battle? He was into his best stuff now, the bit between the shopper and the bag boy, who always seems to put the eggs beneath the gallon tub of Rocky Road, and the final moment of truth, when the bagger asks you if you want paper or plastic? Ladies and gentlemen, let me humbly submit that it is time to answer that timeless question with a new question, whose only query is whether Mother Earth is truly worth saving or whether we're all forever locked into the proverbial roller coaster ride to hell, damned to a cycle of wasteful neglect that is the blight of modern society—he was hitting his stride now, his notes urging him on, begging him not to look away. He wouldn't. He'd ride his own momentum to the end. He could feel it coming on, and grabbed the canvas bag from beneath the podium.

"And so I say," Jacob said, slipping the bag over his head, "environmental destruction—" For a moment Jacob was lost in darkness, until he realized he'd put the bag on backward. He tugged at it with both hands. The bag got stuck on his shirt. Jacob could hear whispers, the first sounds of nervous alarm. He wrestled with the bag, which suddenly felt like it was closing off the air around him.

"Environmental destruction," Jacob repeated, remembering to raise his hands and signal a touchdown. "It's—in the bag!"

Zoe was the first one to tell him about Martin Weaver's death. Martin had been killed in a car accident the night before when his Toyota drifted into an oncoming moving van, which veered just enough to spare the moving-van driver's life, but sent Martin's car into a narrow creek, into which Martin's body had been flung. He'd died instantly, according to Principal Stanton, who'd broken the news to everyone during this morning's announcements. There would be a memorial service on Thursday and a funeral on Friday, he said, before choking up and asking for a moment of silence, which few had honored, the most crying Zoe said she'd ever heard in her life. "It was like we were all crying together, at once," Zoe said, before beginning to cry again. "I don't even know how to describe it." The class had spent their first period talking about their grief. Even Mr. Olsen had cried, right there in the biology lab. "We don't know what's around the corner, do we?" he'd said, and then put his head to his hands. In Mrs. Scheer's class they talked some more, Mrs. Scheer crying, too, before asking them if they'd like to have a free period. Zoe couldn't have been more surprised than when Buddy Hamilton raised his tattooed hand and said they had to go on, to which Mark Gaudry and Mike Hartlett quickly concurred, Mike saying, in a voice choked with tears, "It's what Martin would have wanted."

Jacob received this news in Mrs. Scheer's classroom, which, minutes before, had emptied of Jacob's classmates. They'd passed him by without congratulating him on his outfit, a few of them taking pains to leave the room by exiting the row two rows away from his, when it would have been easier to leave by his row.

Jacob looked at Zoe now, who had begun to cry again. "I was at the dentist," he explained.

Zoe nodded.

"I mean," Jacob said, "there's no way I could have known."

A moment passed in which Zoe could so easily have said of course, there was no way he could have known, of course, no one could argue otherwise. The clock Jacob had spent so many hours idly watching ticked audibly.

"But everybody knew," Zoe said. She wiped a tear away. "Everybody."

"I was at the dentist," Jacob said, the anger in his voice surprising even to him.

"And you wore that stupid outfit," Zoe said. "And made all those jokes when Martin was dead and everyone was thinking about Martin. You put a grocery bag over your head." She began to cry again. "Oh, Jacob, what were you thinking?"

Jacob stood from his desk and tucked the canvas grocery sack inside his book bag. "I was at the dentist," he said.

Zoe looked at him as if he'd shoved her. "What's wrong with you? Martin is dead, Jacob. He's a dead person who is *dead*." She began to cry again.

A few students began entering the room. They glanced at Jacob in his grocery bag outfit, placed their books on their desks, and immediately left the room again.

"You two used to be friends," Zoe sobbed.

Jacob placed his book bag across his shoulders and tightened the straps.

"What's wrong with you, Jacob?" Zoe said. "Don't you even care?"

Jacob put his hands in front of her face, as if to say, *Enough.*

"Don't put your hands in my face," Zoe said. She threw a notebook at him that sailed to the right and landed beneath Mrs. Scheer's desk.

"I was at the dentist," Jacob said.

"Just get away from me," Zoe said. "I don't want to hear your stupid voice."

When Jacob left the room, a crowd of students waited on the other side of the door. They parted quickly, but not before Jacob heard one of them mutter, "That's him right there" and another one whisper, "In the grocery bags." Although Jacob wasn't positive that it was anything more than an accident, he was shoved against a locker. He put his hands against it to brace his fall.

The year before, Jacob had stopped being friends with Martin. They'd started hanging out sophomore year when Martin was kind of dating Sarah Moore and Jacob and Zoe were whatever Jacob and Zoe were. A couple? It was hard to say. They'd done a few things together, had once nearly relinquished their virginity to each other without actually doing so, and lied whenever someone asked them if they were together. *We're just friends,* they'd say, or, *It's nothing serious.*

Zoe was friends with Sarah, so when Sarah and Martin started kind of dating, the four of them kind of began spending time together. Martin was a year older than the rest of them, and had recently acquired his driver's license, along with the occasional use of his older brother's car, an ancient Toyota Tercel that listed to one side whenever the four them managed to squeeze inside, off to McDonald's or the mall or the park where they sometimes sipped cheap wine from a brown bag and drove home again chewing the breath mints Martin's brother kept in the glove compartment. On weekends they'd hang out at Martin's house, watching movies and killing time in Martin's basement, where Jacob pretended to lose game after game of pool to Martin after Zoe had privately berated him for twice running the table, when the game obviously meant so much to Martin, who wasn't very good at most things, and who often served as the butt of jokes among the four of them, no matter how many times Zoe said they had to stop doing that. They didn't stop doing that, but was it really their fault, Jacob always wanted to say, when Martin was the way Martin was?

Martin had once stood on Sarah's porch for thirty-five minutes ringing the doorbell that didn't work, without ever thinking to knock. Martin videotaped himself eating a cheese sandwich to see how he might improve looking cool while chewing and had shown the videotape to Sarah, Zoe, and Jacob to get their feedback, the four of them seated around Martin's television, from which Martin's mouth bulged and chewed and occasionally narrated what he was trying to do, as in "Now I'm trying to eat the crust without making my lips look weird," as the three of them laughed so hard they cried, much to Martin's surprise, who said, dejectedly, "I didn't mean for it to be funny," which was even funnier, and sent Jacob to the floor, clutching his sides. But what Martin did more than anything was force a friendship with Jacob, or so it seemed to Jacob, who quickly began to resent Martin's frequent phone calls, especially when Martin's relationship with Sarah began to sour, as it had in the months leading up to the time Jacob finally stopped being friends with him—if they ever were, that is.

What were they?

Martin would call him for no reason whatsoever, it seemed, right in the middle of dinner or homework, Jacob's mother using the fluty voice she always used whenever Zoe or Martin called, so that it was often hard to tell if the caller was Martin or Zoe until Jacob reached the phone and his mother whispered, "It's Martin."

"Hi Martin," Jacob said, flatly.

"Hey, Budzilla," Martin said.

"Don't call me Budzilla."

"I keep forgetting," Martin said.

"We're eating dinner now."

"I know," Martin said. "Tacos and salad. Your mom told me. Yum."

"I have to finish my dinner."

"I'm feeling kind of down," Martin said, "about Sarah."

"All right," Jacob sighed, and felt the way he always felt when he talked to Martin on the phone, that he was both talking to Martin and somehow listening to himself talk to Martin at the same time. So he both heard and felt he was somehow observing himself hear Martin telling him how he never knew what to say around Sarah anymore, how they spent most of their time driving around in the

Toyota—the Martinmobile, Martin had maddeningly started calling it—trying to think of places to go, but always ended up back at Martin's house, where they pretended to watch TV and made out on the upstairs sofa until they got to a point where it was clear they'd gotten to a point neither one of them had any idea how to act upon, the two of them nearly naked, Martin's parents still lurking around downstairs, Martin's mother theatrically coughing at the bottom of the stairs the moment before she ascended them, one slow step at a time, calling out, "Hope I'm not interrupting anything." They'd zip back into their clothing and not speak to each other for the rest of the night until Martin had to drive Sarah home, where they made out a little bit more again, but without really saying anything.

"It's getting weird," Martin said. "How we don't say anything."

Jacob could hear his mom bringing dessert out. "So say something to her," Jacob said.

"Like what?"

"Like you love her. Duh."

"We said that once," Martin said. "Right around the time we stopped saying things to each other."

"So tell her you don't love her then."

"I don't?"

"How the hell would I know?" Jacob said. "She's your girlfriend."

"I guess."

"Just say whatever is on your mind."

"I guess I could try that," Martin said, as if he wasn't really listening. Why did Martin call him in the middle of Jacob's dinner if he really wasn't going to listen to him anyway?

"I have to go now," Jacob said.

"Do you think you could sort of tell Zoe to tell Sarah to say something to me?" Martin said. "I mean, do you think she would do that?"

"Look," Jacob said, and then realized he had no idea how he was to finish his sentence.

"You wouldn't have to come out and tell her to do it, like a command or something," Martin said, thoughtfully. "You could just sort of mention how nice you think it would be if Sarah talked a little more to me when the two of us are alone together. I could see Zoe saying something like that to Sarah."

"Look," Jacob said.

"And it's not like Sarah would ever figure out that I put you up to it, to telling Zoe," Martin continued. "I mean, I know how much you like Sarah."

Jacob thought Sarah was a horrible snob. She had a cousin who was at Harvard, a fact she tried to introduce into nearly every conversation Jacob could remember having with her. "Look," he said, "Sarah is great. It's just that—"

"I knew you'd be OK with it," Martin said.

"This is a stupid conversation," Jacob said.

"You say that word a lot," Martin observed. " 'Stupid.' "

And the next time Jacob saw Martin, Martin didn't even mention Jacob having hung up on him.

That Thursday Jacob attended the memorial service for Martin. The service was held in the school gymnasium, whose bleachers were lined with students and parents and teachers in long black dresses and coats, their fingers clutching the program Jacob kept reading over and over again to avoid looking around him, to wherever Zoe was. He'd stayed home the day after his presentation; his parents didn't question him. He returned to school the following day, where the hallways still seemed to hold the scent of his humiliation, people he didn't even know giving him looks he couldn't quite read, his teachers treating him like he was someone they'd just met, an unknown quantity, a transfer student, perhaps, not the congenial class clown who'd so often won his classmates' laughter. For most of the day before the memorial service, Jacob spent his time staring down at his textbooks, wondering if he'd lose his classmates' yearbook vote for Funniest, a title he'd held since freshman year, an honor that Jacob now felt he'd squandered away. Jacob looked up from his books in a momentary panic that people could read his thoughts, which they could not, he reminded himself. Thank God they could not.

The service began with a slide show, photographs of Martin in his playpen, a Little League uniform, holding a hooked bass, playing basketball with his older brother, and then showed more recent images: Martin soaping up a car for a fund-raising car wash, Martin posing in his marching band uniform, Martin standing atop the home team bleachers, his hands cupped to his cheering mouth. A song accompanied these images, and it wasn't until Jacob chanced looking around for the song's source that he saw Buddy Hamilton seated at the front of the gymnasium, blowing "Amazing Grace" through his significantly dented saxophone, which caught the gymnasium lights in just such a way that it seemed Buddy was breathing golden fire. Jacob looked away, but not before glancing at the next slide: a photograph of Martin, Sarah, Zoe, and him hanging out in Martin's backyard, Jacob and Martin giving each other finger bunny ears, their mouths drawn up into ridiculous smiles. Jacob recalled Martin's mother saying, "Two comedians here!" as she clicked the photo, a few moments before Jacob had returned to Zoe and whispered, "I'm ready to leave when you are."

Jacob could see Martin's family sitting in the front row, Martin's father holding Martin's mother to his chest, the two of them gently swaying to "Amazing Grace." When the song finished, Principal Stanton approached the podium and thanked everyone for joining together to honor Martin, and then the tributes began, student after teary student, each with a memory to share, each telling the Weavers how sorry they were for their loss, the Weavers nodding, saying thank you, thank you, even, Jacob noticed, Martin's older brother, Jeremy, who'd pinned a photograph of Martin to his suit jacket, and whom Jacob had only met once, on one of Jeremy's rare weekends home from college, when they'd helped Jeremy load his enormous stereo speakers into the Toyota. Sarah Moore tried to say a few words, but broke down after spotting Martin's parents, who stood to help her down from the podium. Mrs. Scheer lightened the mood by recalling the time Martin had risen to her challenge to use as many of the week's new vocabulary words in a single sentence by writing *This week's new vocabulary words are acumen, aggrandize, factotum, hirsute, paean,* etc. "Martin marched to his own drummer," Mrs. Scheer concluded, then sobbed, "he will be very much missed."

Jacob could feel a few eyes upon him as Zoe stepped to the podium. She'd worn the black dress he'd once been permitted to partially remove after one of their sort of dates, and Jacob was embarrassed to find himself aroused in the middle of Zoe's speech, which, although nearly tearless, was the most deeply felt of the evening, with Zoe choking up only once, near the end, when she'd perhaps surprised herself by saying, "All those times I thought I'd tell Martin what a great guy I thought he was, and then suddenly there wasn't any time anymore." Although Jacob would never tell anyone, he heard Zoe's words as if they were about him instead, and felt himself, for the first time that evening, on the verge of tears. "I only wish there was more time," Zoe said, before wiping her tears away. "I'm so sorry, Jacob."

But of course she'd said *Martin*—Jacob scanned the room anyway, just in case, to see if anyone was looking at him.

When the service ended, Jacob kept playing his version of Zoe's speech over and over again. Zoe in her black dress, saying how she regretted not telling him what a great guy he was. How she regretted not having more time to tell him so. *I'm so sorry, Jacob.* Jacob caught up with her just outside the gym doors. Zoe didn't say anything when he fell into step with her as she made her way to the parking lot, where, already, Jacob's classmates seemed to eye him for a moment before climbing into their parents' cars, among which lurked the Ducks Unlimited station wagon, still wearing its terrible bumper sticker and still weeks away from becoming his.

"Hey, Zoe," Jacob said.

Zoe placed her hands in her pockets, from which she withdrew a surprisingly old-fashioned looking handkerchief and wiped her eyes, a gesture Jacob was glad no one knew he found a little maudlin. The handkerchief had tiny white flowers around the edges.

"That was really nice," Jacob said, "what you said."

And it wasn't until Zoe turned to him that Jacob realized he must have been smiling a little. "What's wrong with you, Jacob?" Zoe said.

"Nothing," Jacob stammered. "I just thought it was nice what you said, you know, about Martin."

Zoe's face was puffy, raw. "Aren't you even a little sad?"

"Of course I'm sad," Jacob said. "Of course I am."

"Stop saying 'of course.'"

Jacob threw his hands up in the air. "Jesus! I was only trying to be nice!" he said, a little louder than he intended. Gregory Holdman's family looked his way, Gregory saying something to his parents, who made a pretense of finding their car keys when Jacob returned their gaze. "Why does everyone hate me?"

Zoe balled the handkerchief in one hand and threw it at him all in one motion. "This isn't about you! Why can't you get that through your head? Or is a fucking grocery bag getting in the way?"

Jacob's classroom humiliation returned anew, this time with an image he'd forgotten until now: Mrs. Scheer's look of disgust, the moment Jacob had located the eye holes and peeked through.

"I was at the dentist!" Jacob shouted.

"Don't shout at me," Zoe said.

And she nearly relented when Jacob issued forth a sudden sob. "They were running late," he explained. "My appointment."

Jacob did tell Zoe about Martin's request. They'd both laughed about it, behind Martin's back, poor Martin, wanting Sarah to like him as much as he liked her. It was pathetic, being around them, as Jacob and Zoe often were in the weeks leading up to Sarah and Martin's breakup, which, when it finally arrived, seemed several months overdue. They'd spent those last few weeks driving around in the Martin-mobile, which Martin had recently fitted out with an expensive sound system, from which he played mix CDs whose songs were all testimonies of love, with a predilection for self-pity and self-effacement, a theme none of them would have noticed if Martin hadn't pointed it out to them, over and over again, sometimes lingering at a stop sign for nearly two minutes as the next song reached the chorus, Martin raising a finger, saying, "Listen to this next part. Not this part. Not this part. OK, now. *Listen.*"

That last week before the breakup, Martin called Jacob every night. He didn't know what to do, he said. He felt like Sarah was going to dump him any day now and it was like there was nothing he could do about it. Nothing worked. If he asked Sarah what was wrong, she didn't say anything; if he tried to act like he didn't care, she grew even more distant. It was terrible, Martin said. And then Martin made Jacob promise he wouldn't tell anyone what he was about to tell him next, even Zoe, especially not Zoe, no.

"We did it," Martin said. "I mean we kind of did it one time. But you can't tell anyone, ever."

"Fine," Jacob lied, already planning on calling Zoe later.

"Her parents were away," Martin said. "So we had the place to ourselves. And we kind of agreed that we'd do it—it was Sarah's idea, if you can believe that, not mine. I said there was no pressure. She didn't have to if she didn't want to. But she said we should, so we did. Sort of." Martin lowered his voice. "I mean we started to, but this weird thing happened. To me, I mean. I just got this feeling that if we did it I wouldn't know what to say to her as we were doing it, and I ended up telling her I was scared I wouldn't be able to think of anything to say to her while we were doing it. So we didn't do it," Martin said. "I mean, not really anyway."

"Why would anyone say that?" Jacob said.

"I don't know," Martin said. "I just ended up saying it." Then, "Haven't you ever wondered about that? I mean, I can picture everything about doing it, except what I'll be saying as we're doing it. Do you know what I mean?"

"No," Jacob said, although Martin had just precisely described his most private fear about sex. It was as if Jacob had hidden a small box inside a larger box and placed it on a high shelf and Martin had walked in, reached up to the box, pulled out the smaller box and said, What's *this* all about?

"I thought you'd understand," Martin said.

"You need to chill out around Sarah," Jacob said. "Just relax."

"You know what the most unrelaxing word in the world is?" Martin said. "It's 'relax.'"

And then there was the last time the four of them ever hung out together, the weekend of the crow's nest. Martin's parents were away for the evening, and somehow Martin had gotten hold of some box wine, which they'd carried around Martin's neighborhood, drinking tall cups of cheap red wine, ducking behind bushes whenever a car passed by. They ended up at the neighborhood park where they ascended the crow's nest that topped the children's play area, a small enclosure whose opening was wide enough to admit one of them at a time. It was dark inside the nest, which had a low roof and smelled like damp wood. Jacob was the last one to climb inside. He could barely see the others. Zoe handed him the wine box, from which he took a drink directly from the spout: the first indication that he was, in fact, drunk.

"Yo ho ho," Martin said, and everybody laughed.

They were sitting shoulder-to-shoulder, knees drawn tight, the wine box passing among them now. Zoe and Sarah were making fun of people they all knew, doing mean impersonations of teachers and peers, just the kind of thing Jacob enjoyed on a night like this, with the wine and the stars, appearing now, just beneath the crow's nest roof, the feeling of Zoe pressed close to him sublimely pleasing, a sign, perhaps, that whatever was sort of between them would, in time, become something graspable and real. They'd get together as

Martin and Sarah had, except Jacob wouldn't blow it, like Martin. They'd do it. They'd already been close a few times, and now Jacob could feel, as certainly as he could feel Zoe's shoulder pressed to his, that their time was near. There it was in the breath upon his neck; he leaned toward Zoe. She leaned into him, the two of them, by the odd angles of their cramped bodies, nearly back to back, a position neither of them wished to relinquish. To test her feeling for him, Jacob pressed the weight of his body into hers; Zoe accommodated him, returning his weight with her own. Jacob heard Zoe laugh.

And that's when Jacob realized he hadn't been leaning back into Zoe at all; he'd been leaning into Martin. He turned to face Martin. Martin gave him a look. It was a look Jacob would never forget, no matter how much he tried to do so, a look he'd never tell anyone about ever, a look he longed to get as far away from as he possibly could. Martin smiled, his teeth visible in the moonlight. *I know,* Martin's look somehow said, *I know.*

A week later, Sarah dumped Martin. Martin called Jacob, but Jacob refused to answer his calls, his mom making up excuses. When Jacob saw Martin lingering by his locker, he walked by without stopping, his eyes focused down the hallway on nothing in particular.

Jacob didn't attend Martin's funeral. Zoe said she understood, but Jacob knew she didn't mean it. Everybody went. Well, let them, Jacob thought. What Jacob wanted more than anything was for Martin's death to fade into the past, taking with it all the attendant shows of grief and sorrow and loss. Jacob was glad no one knew how tired he was getting of those, no matter how many times Zoe pressed him about his feelings or brought up his ill-timed speech again. That was the real thing, Jacob wanted everyone to know without actually having them know it: Martin's death had totally eclipsed his speech, which should have gotten some attention, some little show of appreciation, despite everything else that had happened. But he could never say that.

Jacob still got some odd looks from time to time, but eventually people stopped confronting him, as Buddy Hamilton had done the week after the funeral, poking a thick finger into his chest as he gathered his gym clothes together. When Jacob asked what the problem was, Buddy only poked his finger into his chest again, as if that were answer enough. Jacob didn't tell Zoe about it, nor did he tell her about the time someone called his house and screamed "Bag boy!" into the receiver. It would pass, Jacob figured. All he needed to do was relax. Hadn't he once advised someone to relax?

A few months after Martin's funeral, Jacob got his driver's license. He scraped the Ducks Unlimited bumper sticker off his mother's station wagon and drove everywhere and anywhere he could. The feeling of driving! It was amazing how good it felt to cruise through neighborhoods he had only ever biked through before, or join the highway like everyone else, driving to the mall if he wanted to, the supermarket, the chain stores along the frontage road. Zoe seemed to enjoy driving around, too (she would get her license in another two months), and Jacob was now permitted to drive her home from school sometimes, or pick her up on weekends for a movie or a football game.

The station wagon also gave their relationship new room to roam, the two of them making out in the parking lot behind the refinery, or touching each other as Jacob drove—Zoe's willingness to do so surprised Jacob greatly—sometimes without saying a word, the streetlights passing by like pale witnesses. They'd drive around Zoe's neighborhood for an hour, completing several acts of intimacy as Jacob negotiated cul-de-sacs and took speed bumps at a slow crawl, careful not to scrape the station wagon's underside. They explored the backseat, which was roomier than Jacob imagined, all those years of riding back there en route to a soccer game or band practice. And, when they agreed that they were ready for what seemed like the next step, the step the other steps had been so happily winding their way toward, Zoe suggested they try folding down the backseats and using the station wagon's interior for what Jacob had always imagined they'd use it for, even on the afternoon he'd scraped the bumper sticker away.

They were in a company parking lot. It was dark out, but still light enough to see the trees bordering the lot, a few empty cars closer to the building. Zoe folded down the seats while Jacob found the key to open the way back. There was a blanket back there he planned on using, the one they sometimes used when hauling old furniture to the Salvation Army, or for sitting on the grassy sidelines, still wet with dew. Jacob opened the back and grabbed the blanket, which revealed something in the cargo space underneath: the grocery bag outfit, still there since the day of his speech, the sleeves slightly bent, but intact. The pants had been folded, too, careful as a wedding tux.

"What the hell?" Zoe said. She was standing beside him now in the nimbus of light from the car's interior. "Why do you still have that?"

"I guess I forgot about it," Jacob lied, since he'd found it there once before and had nearly thrown it away—but couldn't. Instead, he'd placed the blanket on top.

"I can't believe you'd keep that, Jacob," Zoe said. "How could you?"

"There's nothing wrong with it," Jacob protested.

"Everything is wrong with it! How could you keep something like that?"

But Jacob reached in and grabbed the pants. "Look how I stitched the inseams," he said. "They're really good."

Zoe backed away from him, like he was a zombie in a horror film. "Don't show me that fucking thing," she said.

But Jacob was already slipping the pants on. "The belt is the best part," he said. "No one even noticed the belt."

Zoe called Jacob a name he didn't like. "You're heartless," she said. "You don't give a damn about anything or anyone. You really don't."

But Zoe was wrong. Jacob cared about a great many things, and that's why he fastened the coupon buckle the way it was meant to be fastened, and made sure the grocery bag sleeves didn't get caught on his fingers when he slipped them through. It really was a remarkable outfit, better even than he remembered. Jacob was sad not to have kept the canvas grocery bag back there, too, with the other pieces. If he only had that bag, he might really show Zoe the proper way the suit was to be worn.

SLOW CAR

My junior year of high school, someone stole a vending machine from the gym lobby. The machine was one of those coffee/hot chocolate machines you don't see much anymore, the kind where, for a few coins, a white paper cup descended from behind a Plexiglas door and a sudden stream of brown liquid filled it to the brim. The door often refused to budge. TAKE-A-BREAK, the machine's sign read, although no one would remember that but Chelsea and me.

It wasn't clear why someone would want to steal the TAKE-A-BREAK machine. There were better, more popular machines in the lobby that would have been just as easy, or just as difficult, to steal. The TAKE-A-BREAK machine had to be heavy, we all reasoned, too heavy for one person to move. Some kind of prank, we guessed. Another good-bye from the senior class, who had already painted the faculty parking lot pink and had run every toilet, urinal, sink, shower, and water fountain at exactly 1:47 P.M. on the Wednesday before Christmas break. Although nothing had happened, I always liked to imagine that I felt my desk shake at 1:47 on the Wednesday before Christmas break. I remember looking at Chelsea the moment it happened (we were all in on the prank, all nervous smiles and barely suppressed laughter) as we sat in the middle of Mr. Young's civics class, the clock above Mr. Young's chalkboard festooned with plastic snowflakes. Chelsea had given me a look I've puzzled over since. It was a look that was somehow meant to suggest her disappointment in me, although I could see her glancing at the clock, too, with something like fear. It was the only time I could remember Chelsea looking afraid about anything.

I wasn't popular in high school, but I wasn't exactly unpopular either. I had a respectable grade point average, enough friends to sit with at lunch and pep rallies, and ran cross-country in the winter, although without much success. I could never figure out how to keep my throat from aching after ten minutes out in the cold, the cross-country team circling the community reservoir with our breath pluming before us like cartoon exclamations. My legs felt fine; I could run for miles. But my throat felt raw, on fire. Sometimes I'd chew vitamins while I ran, but they never helped all that much. I ended up quitting the team after my sophomore year, for reasons I can't even remember now.

I'd been hanging out with Chelsea since sophomore year. She'd transferred to our school after her father transferred to work in the chemical plant where nearly everybody else's dad worked, too. My dad had worked there, and so had my mother until my little brother was born. So, the first time I went to Chelsea's house, it was no surprise to see the same company stationery we had next to our telephone, or the same blue and yellow pens I used to write nearly every school assignment, their sides emblazoned with the company logo. Chelsea and I drank soda from company glasses, which left rings on Chelsea's nightstand. I mention these items not to suggest that they tied Chelsea's life to mine, or mine to hers, but only to say that they were the first things I noticed when I entered Chelsea's home, and the sight of them now (I still have a company glass) returns me to those afternoons when Chelsea and I sat at her kitchen table while her mother ran a cloth across the countertop, and a casserole, newly lifted from the oven, breathed steam into the air.

Chelsea's bedroom was the first girl's bedroom I'd ever seen. It had a canopy bed and stuffed animals—it was that kind of bedroom. Chelsea wasn't my girlfriend and I wasn't her boyfriend, but those distinctions didn't seem to carry over into our home lives somehow. School lent a social clarity that our neighborhoods could never quite grasp. Chelsea would sit on her bed and play songs for me on her stereo. I would sit at her desk chair and study the album cover (this was back in the days of LPs). "Well?" she'd say, after a few songs, and I'd tell her I liked it or I wasn't sure or I guess it was OK. I don't remember much about the music, to be honest. But I could tell the music was some kind of test I was failing and failing horribly, even after I said things like, "This is incredible," or "Will you make me a tape?" Half my friendships back then were based upon making somebody else a tape. But Chelsea didn't say anything. She just sat on her bed without comment until the next song started up.

Sometimes her mom would invite me to stay for dinner and her dad would tell corny jokes while I tried to butter bread without tearing it. Her dad was pretty funny. He died a few years ago, or so somebody told me, and I thought about sending Chelsea a card, but I never did. I'd even gotten her address from a friend of a friend, had even filled out the envelope and written the card, even though I knew I wasn't going to send it. Maybe that's why I permitted myself to draw a little vending machine beneath my signature. *Remember?* I'd written.

"This one's an import," Chelsea said, on one of those afternoons when we were hanging out in her bedroom. "From Finland."

"Finland," I said. "Wow."

Chelsea said, "I'm still deciding about this one," and played a song that sounded exactly like the last song. Many of the songs didn't have words, which bothered me. What was the point of songs without words?

"Just think," Chelsea said, about another song I was struggling to get the idea of, "we're probably the only people in the world listening to this song right now."

I looked out Chelsea's window and into the backyard. It was early fall; still warm enough to go without a jacket, but the leaves were already starting to turn. "That's weird," I said. It was just beginning to get dark outside.

I don't know what Chelsea expected me to say about the songs. That they were a kind of test was clear to me, but a test of what? All I knew for certain was that, whatever the correct answers were, I wasn't giving them. I disappointed Chelsea. She wanted something from me I was too dumb to understand. Whatever Chelsea's idea of me was, I knew it was the wrong idea. Or, worse: she knew exactly how empty I was, but thought she could change that. Improve me. *I know what you are,* her music seemed to say, *now let me show you what you might become.* But I knew I'd let her down, eventually. She'd figure out that I wasn't as interesting as she thought and then that would be that.

This was back when I spent a lot of time imagining what other people thought of me. That seemed to be an important thing to think about back then. I tried to be fair, imagining people saying critical things about me in between compliments, whose principal theme, I imagined, was how funny I was without seeming to know it. That was the thing about me, these imagined others would have me know: I didn't even realize how funny I could be. I was one of the funniest people they had ever met and I didn't even know it. But, I imagined someone saying, don't you think he's kind of, I don't know, conceited? Oh no, the others would argue, I think he just comes off that way at first, until you really get to know him. Then you start realizing just how funny he really is.

The last time I hung out with Chelsea we cut study hall and drove to her house in the middle of a thunderstorm. I remember the rain beating against the windshield, which refused to defog, no matter how high Chelsea turned the fan.

"I think you need new wiper blades," I said.

Chelsea rubbed her hand across the windshield. "My dad keeps saying he's going to replace them," she said, "but I don't think he really knows how." She didn't say it with anger, though. That was something I remember liking about Chelsea: she wasn't angry with her parents like everyone else I knew. "One time I found him trying to put the wiper blades on," she said. "He had the owner's manual out across the hood of the car, comparing the replacement blades to the ones in the pictures, I guess. I was going to ask him something, but I ended up just watching him for a while. I was in the garage; he didn't see me. And I just had this horrible feeling that he was going to die someday and there was nothing I could do about it. It was terrible."

I didn't know what to say, so I ended up saying something moronic about wiper blades being really hard to figure out. Chelsea nodded like I had said something helpful, but she didn't speak the rest of the drive.

When we pulled into Chelsea's driveway, Chelsea did something she'd never done before: she pulled the car into the garage. Usually we just parked in the driveway and walked through the front door (a key was hidden beneath a stone turtle). "The rain," Chelsea explained.

"Yeah," I said.

Chelsea navigated the car between a trash can and a hanging bicycle. "I hate this part," she said.

"I know what you mean," I said.

"Sometimes I feel like the rest of my life will be like pulling into my parents' garage," Chelsea said.

After I'd gathered my book bag, I opened my door and noticed something along the far wall of the garage: a blue tarp pulled tightly around a tall oblong object. The object was the approximate size of a refrigerator. The tarp was the kind you throw across a pool in winter, a loose, crinkly thing that had been secured with bungee cords. The cords were so peculiar looking, each hooked into another like a dozen clasped hands, that I found myself looking at the object a few beats longer than I might have normally, after my eyes had processed what they saw as a spare refrigerator strangely wrapped in a blue tarp, to what a longer glance now revealed: the TAKE-A-BREAK machine, here, in Chelsea's garage.

"Is that the TAKE-A-BREAK machine?" I said.

Chelsea followed my gaze. "I don't want to talk about the TAKE-A-BREAK machine," she said.

"How did you get it here?" I could feel my voice turning into my excited voice. "How did you do it? I mean . . . there's just no way that you could have."

Chelsea gave me a look. It was the same look she turned on me when I said that a song sounded "really cool."

"Leave your shoes by the door," she said.

But I wouldn't give up. I unlaced my sneakers, all the while pounding Chelsea with questions. Did her older brother help her? Was she planning on giving it back? Had she managed to get the money out of it? How much was there? Did the machine still work? Why, why, why had she done it? But Chelsea didn't say anything. She took off her shoes and left them next to mine. They were the same kind of sneakers I wore, something I hadn't noticed until now, except that Chelsea had switched out the white laces for black ones. They looked much better that way. Cooler. I would never think to do anything like that. I still don't do anything like that. Sometimes I'll catch myself driving behind a slow car for miles and miles, and then realize I could have passed it easily enough. I'll speed by in the left-hand lane, feeling like I'm getting ahead, and then find myself following behind another slow car later on.

That afternoon we sat in Chelsea's kitchen and ate grilled cheese sandwiches. The kitchen table faced out onto the backyard, where I could see puddles forming on the patio Chelsea had once asked me to sweep, for no reason that I can remember now. I had done as she asked, making a joke of it later, although I thought it was a strange thing to ask someone to do. Why couldn't she do it herself? Anyway, I looked out the window and remembered the feeling of the broom in my hands, the simple pleasure I took in sweeping the patio, where dry leaves clung to the concrete and the patio furniture required moving, navigating the broom underneath the table a sudden game I was glad to master. We watched the rain for a while. Chelsea ate her grilled cheese; I ate mine. It was OK sitting there at the table watching the rain and eating grilled cheese.

What must have happened next is that we went upstairs to Chelsea's bedroom, but I don't really remember going upstairs. Usually her parents would say hello to us while we were hanging out in the kitchen, or Chelsea's dad would shout a hello from the basement if he was down there. I kind of looked forward to that. You could hang out forever in my house without anyone saying hello if they were in another room. My family has never been especially friendly, but we're not unfriendly, either, just not the kind of people who come downstairs from folding laundry to ask you if you'd like something to drink. What I remember about that afternoon in the rain is that Chelsea's parents didn't say hello to us because they weren't home. And I realized that their saying hello was always a kind of tacit permission for us to go upstairs and hang out in Chelsea's bedroom. Yes, you may, their greetings seemed to say. It's fine with us. I remember realizing that and feeling strange. Nervous.

We sat in Chelsea's room and listened to music. Chelsea gave me a mix tape. "For your trip," she said. (I was going away for a long weekend to my grandparents' place in Maryland, where I ended up throwing the tape away, something I've regretted ever since.) I told Chelsea thanks and made a pretense of looking over the song titles, which Chelsea had written in her large, loopy script. Later we looked through old yearbooks and made a game out of cutting out celebrities' heads from magazines and taping them to the shoulders of classmates we disliked. Usually I liked that sort of thing, but the day of the rain I couldn't really get into it somehow. I kept feeling like I was on stage, but I'd never read the script.

What happened next is that we must have started talking about a dress. Either there was a dress in one of the magazines or one sitting on the bed or something like that. I don't really remember. What I do remember is that I was sitting on Chelsea's bed and Chelsea was sitting next to me and the yearbooks and the magazines were splayed around us when Chelsea started talking about a dress.

"I've got a bad dress," she said.

"A bad dress?"

Chelsea nodded. "I never wear it." She flipped through one of the magazines. "It's too bad."

"What's so bad about it?" I remember asking, although I feel dumb admitting that now.

Chelsea shrugged. "Several things," she said. She made a show of reading a long interview with a celebrity I didn't recognize. After a while, the music stopped, but Chelsea didn't get up to put something else on. She just sat on the bed reading the interview like I wasn't really there. I picked up a different magazine, flipped through the pages.

"Do you want to see it?" Chelsea asked.

"The dress?"

"The dress," Chelsea said. But she was still reading the magazine.

"OK," I said. "I mean, if you want."

A moment later Chelsea stood from the bed and went into her closet. A huge walk-in closet crammed with clothes. Chelsea grabbed the dress—it was black, was all I could tell—and walked to the bathroom, closed the door. It was quiet in the room; I could hear her changing. When she opened the door again, I saw Chelsea in the dress. It was one of those little black dresses you've seen so many times you can't remember when was the first time you ever saw one—except for me. Because this was the first time I'd ever seen a dress like that. Ever. I don't want to sound dumb about the way Chelsea looked in that dress, but I remember the way I felt as Chelsea crossed the room and sat down next to me: like I'd just been handed the script, and the next few moments of my life depended on what was inside.

"It's nice," I said, but Chelsea didn't say anything. She picked up the magazine and began reading it again like nothing was different. But she was leaning next to me in a way she wasn't before she put the dress on. I could feel the heat of her body next to me. I could see the outline of her breasts behind the fabric. And then Chelsea put her head on my shoulder.

"You don't like my music," she said.

"Yes, I do," I lied.

"No, you don't."

"I like some of it."

"You just pretend," Chelsea said. I felt the top of her head against my cheek. "You think that makes you a nice person."

"No, I don't."

"You think everyone is a nice person," she said. She gave a little laugh. "But you think you're even nicer." Chelsea must have been sitting right alongside me, because what happened next depended on it: she swung her legs across my body. Right across my lap. And I know how dumb and stupid this sounds, but I didn't think anything of it. I just put my hand on Chelsea's legs like doing so was the most normal thing in the world.

"I don't think I'm nicer," I said, but as soon as I said it, I knew it was a lie. I did think I was nicer. Better, somehow.

"You have a very high opinion of yourself."

Doesn't everyone? I wanted to say. But instead I said, "Not really." I noticed that I was stroking Chelsea's bare legs, as lightly as possible, moving over her thighs, to her knees, her shins—when had I started doing that?

"You do. You really do," Chelsea said. "You think you're Mr. Nice Guy."

I let my hand travel across Chelsea's legs. "I don't think I'm Mr. anything," I said.

"Mr. Sensitive," Chelsea laughed. "Mr. Likeable."

"I'm not Mr. Likeable."

"Mr. Everybody."

"No."

All this time I was moving my hand across Chelsea's legs without either of us saying anything about it. It was the strangest thing. When I moved my hand close to the hem of the black dress, Chelsea shifted her body so that I could move underneath it. I kept expecting someone to walk in. What would someone think, watching this guy move his hand along the legs of this oddly overdressed girl? What would I think if I saw that?

After a while, Chelsea said, "You'll be popular in college. Everyone will like you." College was something we hadn't really talked about. It was still a year away, but already I had plans of going somewhere prestigious, and then returning for the holidays, where I'd bask in everyone's admiration.

"I haven't really thought about that yet," I lied. I was making little circles around Chelsea's knees. Her legs were smooth, warm.

"Everyone will say, 'Oh, he's such a good guy!'" Chelsea laughed, but I didn't get what was funny. I moved my hand across her calves and didn't say anything. It was still raining outside, but you could tell it wasn't really going to last. It was one of those late spring thunderstorms that turn the sky an eerie green, but passes before you even notice it's gone. I looked out the window where I could see trees with their leaves turned up, the way trees sometimes do when it rains. I allowed my hand to move beneath the dress a few times. That seemed like an OK thing to do now.

And then—nothing happened. Zilch. Zero. The end. Chelsea stood from the bed and made her way to the doorway. "Come on," she said, and I gave her a look that intended to say, Why not come back to bed? but Chelsea only motioned me to follow. So that's what I did. I followed.

The garage was still damp from the rain, where our shoes sat side by side. Chelsea stepped over them and walked to the object wrapped in the blue tarp. She began unfastening the bungee cords. "Don't be so sensitive," she said, "give me a hand with these." And I did. I unloosened the cords and let them fall to the ground where they lay like dead snakes. Then I helped Chelsea pull the tarp away. "Ta-da," Chelsea said.

It was the TAKE-A-BREAK machine. I ran my hand over the drink selections. Square buttons with photographs of coffee, hot chocolate, tea. "I can't believe it," I said, but I felt dumb saying it. "It was you."

Chelsea crouched down and plugged the machine into an outlet. "Watch," she said. The machine made a sudden thrumming noise. The drink buttons lit up. I'd never noticed how lovely the TAKE-A-BREAK machine was before. "Does anybody else know?" I asked. "Tell me how you did it."

Chelsea stood next to me and regarded the drink selections like they were something important. Like choosing the right drink was a matter of extreme consequence. She didn't answer me; she pressed a button.

"Tell me," I said.

But Chelsea only lifted a cup to my hands. The cup was full, the liquid not quite hot.

"Here," she said. "Drink this."

Coffee. Weak, but still tasty nonetheless. The TAKE-A-BREAK machine was able to do something with the sweetener that I've never tasted since, although I keep searching. I still get teased today about it, my love of vending machine coffee. How can you drink that? my wife will say, after I've found the rare machine at a bus station or tire shop. They've still got them at some places, but you've got to look. Tire shops are good for them. Car dealerships, too.

"It's good," I said.

Chelsea pressed a button and the machine performed its ritual again, this time leaving a foamy cup of hot chocolate behind the glass door.

"Magic," Chelsea said.

"Yeah."

I took another sip. The coffee seemed warmer since the last time I tasted it, although I knew this wasn't possible. The coffee must have been hotter than I remembered; somehow the idea of watching Chelsea plug the machine in convinced me the coffee would be cold, no matter what it actually tasted like. How easily I could trick myself into thinking something was something it wasn't.

After a while Chelsea said, "You won't hang out with me next year." But there was no accusation in her voice.

"What?"

"You won't," Chelsea said. "It's obvious."

"I can't believe you'd say that," I said, even though I knew Chelsea was right. We wouldn't hang out next year. We'd see each other in the hallways, maybe have a few classes together, but we'd never do anything like this again. And, as soon as I realized this, I felt relieved, set free. "I don't know what you want me to say."

Chelsea shrugged. "If something's obvious you don't have to say anything," she said.

I felt as if I were riding behind a car I could not pass, didn't know how to pass, would never pass, ever.

"You're going to have your best year, next year," Chelsea said. "It's going to surprise you, how good it is. You won't believe it. You'll be amazed. You'll look back and think how it was the best year of your life." She said this as plainly as if she were foretelling that I'd eat breakfast tomorrow or watch some TV.

"Yeah, right," I said.

"You'll stop pretending," Chelsea said.

"Pretending?"

"To be nice."

"Oh," I said.

"You'll see," Chelsea said.

And she was right: it was a great year. Incredible. I sentimental-ized it for as long as it would let me, kind year; long enough, even, to eclipse all those afternoons when I'd hung out in Chelsea's bedroom listening to songs I could never possibly like, would never like, songs that would be the farthest thing from the person I was becoming would ever in a million years listen to. The person I was becoming—whoever that was. I'm embarrassed to think of that person now, so I do not think of that person now. I've passed that person without so much as a glance in the rearview mirror.

Except for this: sometimes, when Chelsea and I were going up-stairs, there would be a moment before we entered her bedroom where Chelsea would turn to see if I was following her, like that might be something in doubt. She'd give me this look—I can still re-member the look Chelsea gave me on the stairs, more indelible than any of those songs—like I was someone she didn't quite want com-ing upstairs with her after all, a sudden stranger following her into her bedroom, someone who wished her harm, even. This boy was lumbering up the stairs behind her, sixteen and in need of an iron. His hair was poorly cut, his teeth not quite straight, his grades aver-age, his friends dull, and his conversation redundant. Three times already he said thanks for a sandwich she didn't even want and had offered off her plate. He climbed the stairs without looking around, without ever mentioning once, not once, how the hallway chande-lier made the ceiling look like it was raining electricity. Instead, he reached the top like he was running from something, a little out of breath. His shirt was redolent of Speed Stick. Who was this boy?

"Hey," he was saying, "wait for me."

TRAGIC LITTLE ME

Leaf wasn't really allowed into Studio Art I, but Mr. Ware insisted. Leaf had Mr. Ware last year for Drawing I, her first unhappy try at being a freshman, although she'd gotten an A in that class. She'd failed every other course, including gym. Now she was fifteen and a freshman again. It wasn't a big deal, except for how it totally was. It was the sun, moon, and stars of her disappointing life. Unless you counted her mother moving back in with her, as she had done the week before school began—then it was only the sun, moon, and most of the stars of her disappointing life.

This morning Leaf sat listening to Mr. Ware criticize a student, Alex, inviting the other students to gather around an easel, where an acrylic of a dog jumping a fence hung from two thick pieces of masking tape. Soon Mr. Ware would ask Leaf for her opinion, and she'd have to say something, Leaf the class pet, as everyone knew. How long was it going to take Mr. Ware to realize that he was making her life worse than it already was?

"Leaf?"

Had someone asked her a question? Of course someone had asked her a question—Mr. Ware, you idiot—he wanted to know what she thought about this dog jumping a fence.

"Leaf? Let's hear your voice today."

Oh, so he wanted to let everyone know that she hadn't talked enough today. Well, she hadn't talked at all today. Why was this dog jumping a fence?

"I guess maybe I don't get the dog," she said.

"Again. This time audibly, please."

"I said I guess maybe I don't get the dog," Leaf said. She could see Alex smile, the way he always did when Mr. Ware reviewed his stuff. In Drawing I last year he'd drawn a series of robots Mr. Ware was always criticizing. "Robots?" he'd said. "All straight lines. I don't want to see you draw another straight line again. And leave the robots to Hollywood. Where they belong."

Mr. Ware walked closer to Alex's painting. "You mean to tell me this thing is a dog?" he said. He put his finger to the dog. "This thing?"

Leaf nodded. A few of the other students laughed.

"So what don't you get about this dog, Leaf?"

"Well," Leaf began, knowing that whatever she said would be wrong. That was how Mr. Ware worked: he made it seem like he was asking your opinion when really he was just waiting to assert his own. It was an approach Leaf usually distrusted in other teachers, but it was hard not to enjoy Mr. Ware's praise. Why was everything so confusing? "I mean, I like that the dog is jumping over the fence. You know, sort of like he's a dog-horse or something." Leaf felt herself on the verge of losing an argument whose terms weren't known to her. And she felt immediately foolish after concluding, "It's like an interesting juxtaposition"—one of Mr. Ware's catchphrases. Already she could see a few of the other students nudging one another. Melanie Worth rolled her eyes at Julie Gregg.

"An interesting juxtaposition?" Mr. Ware said. "Is there an echo in here?" The other students laughed; Leaf felt her face grow warm. "Do you really think so, Leaf, or are you just saying that because Alex is your friend?"

Oh, he's not my friend, Leaf almost said. Then, "I think it's a neat idea?" Her voice went up at the end the way it did when she felt nervous—her grandmother, Miriam, was always on her about that.

"Leaf thinks it's a neat idea, Alex," Mr. Ware said, flatly. "What do you think about that?"

"I can die happy," Alex said, and people laughed.

Mr. Ware said, "Can you really, Alex?" and everyone got that dread sense they got when Mr. Ware was about to go into one of his Speeches that made you feel terrible and embarrassed and angry, no matter how many times you imitated it at lunch for anyone who would listen.

"Can you really die happy now, Alex? Because I don't think you can," Mr. Ware said, "when you know this painting is bullshit." That was another of Mr. Ware's moves: he cursed in class. Leaf couldn't stand that, but other students gobbled it up. She saw a few of them nodding their foolish heads. What an easy crowd.

"But Leaf likes my bullshit," Alex protested with a smile. "She thinks it's interesting."

"Does she really, though? Come on, Alex. What's your Spidey sense telling you, man?"

Everybody laughed. "Hmm, let's see," Alex said. "It's telling me that Leaf thinks my painting is bullshit?"

"You're asking me what your Spidey sense is telling you?" Mr. Ware said. "Whoa, Spidey, maybe we should give this case to Batman."

By now a few of students were laughing so hard that Mr. Ware had to raise his hands to quiet them down. "Try again, Spidey."

"OK. My painting sucks?"

"Closer. Keep going."

"My painting sucks hard?"

"It's getting warm in here," Mr. Ware said.

"My painting sucks super-hard?"

"Almost there."

"Um, my painting sucks donkey balls?"

That got everyone. Michael Young dropped to his knees and laughed noiselessly; Meghan Green held her hands to her face, saying, I can't believe he said that! Leaf felt the attention turn away from her, but there was no relief in it. Mr. Ware raised his hands again until everyone quieted down.

"Donkey balls?" Mr. Ware said. "Now those would be interesting. What would donkey balls look like? How would you paint them?" He circled the easel. "First, you'd have to find some donkey balls. That would be the first step, right? Leaf, wouldn't you say that would be step numero uno?"

"OK," Leaf said.

"And what do you think the second step might be, after you've found yourself some first-class, grade-A donkey balls? Alex?"

"Paint them?" Alex guessed.

"Leaf, did you hear that," Mr. Ware said, without looking at her. He was walking to a nearby window that looked out onto the faculty parking lot and the football field. "Your buddy Alex says that step two would be to paint those donkey balls. What color, Alex?"

"Uh, maybe yellow ocher?" Alex said.

"Yellow ocher, Leaf." Mr. Ware looked out the window. The sky was gray, free of comfort. "Paint those donkey balls yellow ocher. That sound like step two to you?"

She didn't know why he set her up this way. "I don't know," she mumbled. Sending her beneath the basket for an easy alley-oop. "I guess not."

"Oh no? What would step two be in your book?"

Leaf felt the ball in her hands. Go ahead, shoot. "Maybe . . . looking?" she said.

"Looking?" Mr. Ware said. "Like the way I'm looking out this window?"

"Yes," Leaf said.

"You mean to tell me you'd like to look at those donkey balls before you start painting them?"

Leaf nodded. She could feel her classmates' contempt gathering around her. A sensation like strangers crowding around you on a packed bus.

"What do you think, Alex? Leaf says step two equals look."

"I'm with Leaf," Alex said.

"Are you?" Mr. Ware said, and people laughed.

"I am."

"Because I don't see any looking in this dog painting," Mr. Ware said. He was standing by the painting again, regarding it with what seemed renewed disgust. "You know what I see here? I see an idea. Want to know what the idea is? The idea is a dog jumping over a fence. See it? But, know something? This painting isn't even a dog jumping over a fence. Do you know what it is? Leaf?" He turned to her and saw that she wasn't going to answer him. "I'll tell you what it is," he said. "It's the *idea* of a dog jumping over the *idea* of a fence." Mercifully, the bell rang—had there ever been a more merciful bell than that one? No, Leaf decided, there had not. "Your paintings could care less about your ideas for them," Mr. Ware said, as the class packed their supplies away and threw their brushes into jars brimming with dirty water. "Lose your ideas."

When Leaf was zipping up her book bag, Mr. Ware signaled her over. He was sitting at his drafting table, pouring a cup of coffee from the coffeemaker he kept there: you were allowed to drink from it if you brought your own cup, changed the filter, and didn't tell "the administration" about it.

Mr. Ware took a sip of coffee from the same Styrofoam cup Leaf noticed him using yesterday. She always noticed dumb things like that. "Listen, when I do that kind of stuff I did today, I do it for a reason, OK?"

Leaf nodded.

"I do it because I've got a bunch of kids in here who are just passing through, like tourists. They should be wearing little hats and sunglasses."

"Oh," Leaf said. "I get it."

"Do you? Because I was just about to ask you what the hell I'm talking about." He gave her a look that suggested he was joking. "OK, what I'm trying to say is that you are not a tourist. You're a lifer. Like it or not."

"Oh," Leaf said. Then, "Thanks."

"There are about twenty mistakes every beginning artist makes," Mr. Ware continued, "and you're not making any of them."

"Thanks."

"You're probably the best student I've seen in years."

"Thanks."

"Anyway, there's an open house two weeks from this Thursday, and I wonder if you'd like to display some of your work. I'm supposed to pick three students. You're all three, but I'll find two others for ballast."

"Wow, thanks," Leaf said.

"Is that a yes?"

"OK."

"OK equals yes?"

"Yes."

"Great," Mr. Ware said.

On the days when Leaf didn't feel like going home to her grandmother's, she walked to The Winner's Circle, the restaurant where her mother worked. It was a long walk, but Leaf liked the feeling of being on her own, if only for a walk through a college town, where cars full of boys sometimes slowed beside her and asked things she would never repeat to anyone. Things she understood but pretended not to. Sometimes Leaf pretended to be younger than she actually was. Pretending helped keep a lighter, more innocent version of herself aloft; a version that was most pleasing to Miriam and her mother, especially her mother, who wore her fears of inadequacy as plainly as the name tag on her Winner's Circle uniform.

Leaf had lived with Miriam since she was six years old. Miriam had raised her, while Leaf's mother and father lived across town in a house Miriam had purchased for them—something she brought up whenever her anger rose, as it often did whenever Leaf's mother was around. And now she was around all the time, moving in with them while she separated from Leaf's father, although she wouldn't say as much. But Leaf knew. Soon her mom would find her own place, and she'd be like half the kids in her class, dividing holidays and weekends, dropped off at the curb in one car, picked up in another. Sometimes, when no one was around, Leaf would whisper "divorce," trying to give herself a shock, but she didn't feel anything, really. Saying "divorce" was no different than saying "hello" or "melba toast." This depressed her.

Leaf found her mother in the restaurant's kitchen. She was seated with Gloria, the owner, folding napkins into triangles, something Leaf used to enjoy, but no longer did. No longer cute little Leaf, the quiet child, drawing unicorns on placemats, although her hair was still as long as ever, and seemed to keep adulthood at bay.

"Gets longer every time I see you," Gloria said. She took Leaf's hair and pretend-tied it into a braid. "Rapunzel, Rapunzel."

"Let down your hair," Leaf offered, too quiet to be heard.

"Who you hiding from in there?"

"Me," her mother said.

"Or all her boyfriends," Gloria said.

"Oh, she's smarter than that," her mother said.

"That's good," Gloria said.

"Tell Gloria you're smarter than that," her mother said.

"She doesn't need to say it when I know it," Gloria said.

"I'm smarter than that," Leaf said, obligingly.

"She said it anyway," Gloria said.

Leaf got herself a soda from the fountain, the way she always did. God, she loved getting a soda from the fountain. She was glad no one knew how much she loved getting a soda from the fountain—it was ridiculous. When she returned, Gloria was gone and her mother was smoking a cigarette. When did her mother start smoking again?

"About two weeks now," her mother said.

Leaf didn't say anything.

"Did I know you were coming here?"

"I tried to call you on your cell," Leaf explained. This was true, although she knew her mother wouldn't receive her call: that morning she saw her mother's cell phone resting on the floor next to the sofa where she had left it after falling asleep to a *Road Rules* marathon on MTV. The phone was one of those older ones that didn't fold up like the one Miriam had gotten her, but who was she to say. Everyone else she knew was upgrading to iPhones or Blackberrys, texting in the middle of class. Leaf had never sent a text in her life, practically a misdemeanor for a fifteen-year-old.

"I left it at home," her mother said.

"Oh."

Her mother was folding the napkins with a practiced ease: she could ask Leaf how her day was—what did she learn in school today, ha ha—while smoking and folding at the same time.

"I don't know," Leaf said. "Same old, I guess."

"That's one of those questions you're never supposed to ask your kids," her mother said.

"Really?"

She nodded. "It's in all the books. Your dad used to get on me about it. But what else am I supposed to ask? Maybe he had a point, though. It is kind of a lame question, isn't it?"

Leaf, who had already felt her stomach tighten at the past tense mention of her father, said, "I guess."

"No one can remember what they learned today. It's like asking someone what they dreamed about the night before. Who remembers?"

Leaf said, "Yeah."

"I dreamt I was in a train station, except it wasn't a train station; it was my house, but I knew it was really a train station."

"Yeah."

"That's the way all my dreams are," her mother said. "Nothing is happening but I know something is really messed up and wrong anyway. Like I'm standing in our driveway and I suddenly understand that I'm the last person on earth. Well, not that. I've never dreamed that, actually. Not exactly that, but—do you know what I mean?"

"Kind of."

"Do you?"

"Yeah."

"Do you think I'm a terrible conversationalist?"

"No."

"I do. I can never pay attention to what the other person is saying. Not for long anyway. And if they start saying things I have no idea about, I just pretend that I know exactly what they mean."

"I think like, everybody does that," Leaf said.

"Think so?"

"Sometimes."

Her mother stopped folding and put the cigarette out. "You know what I really can't pay attention to? When someone starts describing their apartment to me. Like, 'First you walk in and there's this little landing and then there's a set of stairs leading to the kitchenette and dining area, and then there's a sunken living room off to the left and a shared bath at the end of the hallway'—I just stop paying attention."

"Yeah."

"Can you pay attention to that?"

"I don't know," Leaf said.

Her mother laughed. "Sometimes I think there's something wrong with me."

Leaf sensed her mother's familiar need for consolation, to say she was a good mother, or at least a mother who didn't have something wrong with her. "Naw," Leaf heard herself say. But I will never be anything like you, she thought.

"But maybe everyone else is paying attention and I'm not. That would be terrible, wouldn't it?"

"I guess."

"It would be like all those dreams I never have. I'm standing in our driveway and suddenly I understand that I'm the only person who doesn't pay attention to what other people say."

Leaf said, "That would be a bad dream."

"A nightmare."

"You'd wake up."

"Screaming."

They sat that way for a while, her mother folding napkins and Leaf drinking soda. The kitchen was quiet this time of day, the dinner rush hours away. After a while her mother said, "I'll give you a ride home."

"Gloria can," Leaf offered. Leaf enjoyed getting a ride home from Gloria, who blasted AM radio and refused to use her wipers in the rain. "Better off without," she'd say, the town beyond the windshield growing exotically dark, headlights transformed into white blooms.

"Gloria's busy," her mother said.

The ride home: an assemblage of awkward, soul-draining silences loosely fitted around her mother's one-sided observations. "You don't see many station wagons around anymore," or, speaking of the driver frozen at the green light ahead of them, "driving is about the seventh thing that woman is doing right now," or, watching a gray squirrel scurry across the median, "your grandmother is terrified of those— did you know?" or, regarding the new town houses creeping up along Mackey Avenue, "supposedly they've got a serious mold problem."

One of the problems of having Sadie as your mother was that you never got around to telling her something you'd actually been meaning to tell her, but couldn't get a word in edgewise, and eventually forgot to mention. Like how Leaf actually wanted to answer her mother's question, what did she learn in school today? Well, several things. She learned there was an open house coming up, and she was invited to show some of her art, at Mr. Ware's request (her mother always seemed to forget who Mr. Ware was, although he was the only teacher Leaf even rarely mentioned). She learned that she was failing history again. Plus algebra. She learned that she was lonelier than she imagined (a girl who had been, of late, giving off a whiff of friendship, was in fact exuding a daily need to borrow a pen). She learned that the bottom lip was the hardest part of the human face to draw. She learned that she could, by angling her head just so, curtain an entire side of a lunch table from view, so that a fruit salad could be eaten in private.

"And you never really get the sense that she can follow a conversation all that well. Like the other night after you went up to bed? We started watching some talk show, some completely terrible late-night talk show, I don't even know who the host was—" were they talking about watching TV? When had Leaf stopped paying attention?

"—and I said, 'Mom, that's the whole point. That's why they're so angry in the first place.' But she just looked at me like I was criticizing her or something, you know the way she gets—"

Oh, she was talking about Miriam. Big surprise, Leaf thought. Lay low.

"Does she ever get that way with you? Does she ever make that little wounded-angry face?"

"I don't know," Leaf said.

"See? I don't think she does with you. Just with me."

Roll over. Play dead.

"You'd know it if she did. You'd know that face anywhere."

"Probably."

"Once you see it, you don't forget."

Nod. Just a little. There.

"That little wounded-angry face. God, I can see it now."

Leaf didn't say anything.

"Know what the funny thing is? The funny thing is I always feel like I'm going to laugh whenever she makes her wounded-angry face. Don't tell. Like the feeling that you're going to crack up during a funeral? Same feeling."

Leaf said that was funny, even though she didn't think it was.

"She needs to get someone to start doing the yard for her at least," her mother said.

They'd pulled up into the driveway. The yard needed mowing, even though it was fall. "Thanks for the ride," Leaf said, and opened the car door. Sometimes Leaf felt guilty for rejecting her mother's offers of girl talk, of agreement, of commiseration, but she didn't know how to accept them when they came with a rider of attacking Miriam.

"You never told me why you didn't take the bus home," her mother said.

Leaf shrugged. "The bus is boring."

"The bus is boring. But I'm not? Is that it?"

"I don't know."

"There was no other reason?"

Leaf shook her head, allowing her hair to shield one eye.

"Well, there doesn't have to be a reason," her mother offered.

Leaf nodded.

"Does there?"

Leaf said, "No."

"OK," her mother said, as if something between them had been at last resolved. "See you tonight."

"Bye." Leaf stood from the car and entered the house, where her grandmother was sitting in an armchair, where she'd just been watching them, no doubt, from a front window. She greeted Leaf by saying, "Talks just to hear her head rattle, doesn't she?"

Leaf's father worked at the university library, where he'd worked since her parents were in school together. Of all the things that Leaf could not imagine, like drowning or walking across hot coals or world peace, her parents' courtship was the thing she could not imagine the most. Yes, they had both been drinkers, smokers, partiers, like nearly everyone else, and yes, they'd met at Wilburstock, the town's sad imitation of Woodstock, where they danced in mud and shared pulls of warm beer while stoned cover bands assaulted the classic rock canon, and yes, they'd both been English majors, but, still, Paul and Sadie? Leaf has seen pictures of her mother and father at this event (they returned every year), her mother wearing, predictably, a tie-dyed T-shirt and cutoffs, her father's pleasure in his newly grown beard as radiant and obvious as the can of Piels raised to the camera.

They'd married their junior year—the *first married couple they knew,* as Leaf has been reminded more than she'd like to be—and lived in so many different apartments and town houses that Leaf has long ago stopped looking whenever her mother or father, driving her through town, slowed the car in front of some pathetic-looking house and said, "That's where we lived when you were one," or, of another depressing duplex, "that's where you found the squirrel in the fireplace," as if to summon Leaf's nostalgia for a time she could not remember. She preferred not to think of the years before they moved into their house, even though the house brought little consolation, a tiny two-bedroom rancher still within striking range of the college's misery, where their lawn was freckled weekly with beer cans, and pizza coupons hung from bright rubber bands wrapped around their doorknob.

It seemed a mistake to Leaf to live in a college town when you were no longer in college. Her mother had dropped out her senior year, although Leaf never knew why. Growing up in a college town had robbed college of all mystery and interest, along with giving her the uncomfortable feeling that her parents' past was somehow lurking behind every building, every shopping center, every new coffee bar ("that's where the diner used to be"), every tree-lined avenue sending long shadows across the sidewalks where her mother and father had stumbled home from so many drunken parties, and where Leaf had later traveled in a stroller purchased by Miriam, whose face looking down into her own is her first memory of her grandmother, the two of them killing time until her mother and father returned from their embarrassing jobs and sent Miriam back to her house, where Leaf longed to go. A college town threw its enlightened arms open to everything, except childhood. There was something uneasy about riding one's pink bicycle through the quad where no one else's training wheels had just been shorn, and where no one else had a grandmother applauding them from the too-green lawn.

Some days Leaf would visit her father and find him in the stacking room. The "cage," everyone called it. Your father's down in the cage, Leaf, someone would say, spotting her hanging out by the periodicals, or checking her email in the computer lab, where she wasn't supposed to be. Leaf would mumble thanks, endure a few appreciative comments about her hair, and then find her father seated at a long table that once sat in the reading room, junked for the newer ones with their AC outlets and Ethernet ports.

"Surprise," she said, visiting him a few days before the school open house. He was checking something on his computer and drinking coffee from a cup Leaf had made him in second grade.

"Hi, sweet pea."

"What are you doing?" Leaf asked.

"Work stuff," her father said. "Boring."

"Oh."

After a while her father said, "I hear I'm going to see some of your art." He gave an encouraging look. "Open house, right?"

"It's no big deal," Leaf said.

"Well, how can it be," her father said, "when it's a huge deal?"

Leaf shrugged.

"Are you going to tell me about it, or do I have to wait?"

Leaf said, "Wait."

"Not even a hint?"

"They're portraits," Leaf said. "Self-portraits." She'd started them last year, in Drawing I, but had never gotten around to finishing them. "Keep going," Mr. Ware had written on her final portfolio. "You're not done here." And she wasn't, she knew, but it wasn't until she started fooling around with charcoals over the summer that where she should be going revealed a little bit of itself to her. She'd pulled her hair into a tight ponytail and sketched her face as it looked without her hair hanging in the way. She'd drawn her portrait as a single line, never lifting the charcoal from the page. The line voided the pupils from her eyes. The line transformed her jaw into a hinge, her ears into half-moons harboring shadowy G clefs. Leaf drew dozens of portraits, gradually loosening the ponytail and letting her hair come back into view. The last portrait, drawn with the aid of a mirror Mr. Ware loaned her as she sat in his office, showed Leaf with her hair fully shielding her face. Up close, you could see her eyes, just barely.

Just barely. That's about how well Leaf felt she understood what she was doing.

"Five years," Mr. Ware said, regarding the portrait. "Can you imagine where your talent will be in five years?"

Leaf, calculating, could not imagine anything about being twenty. The age when her parents had married.

"Or in ten," Mr. Ware said. He took the sketchbook from her and flipped through a few of the portraits. "I wouldn't last one minute in the ring with you in ten years." He laughed. "I'd be on the ropes."

Leaf had stayed after school to work on the portraits. Mr. Ware let her use his office while he worked detention duty in the cafeteria. "Oh," she said.

"It's all ahead of you," Mr. Ware said, and Leaf noticed, for the first time, it seemed, that it was beginning to get dark outside Mr. Ware's office window. How had that happened? Mr. Ware stood in front of his desk, flipping through the sketchbook. He was wearing the same button-down shirt he always wore, the front pocket bulging with the pack of menthols he often produced in the middle of class, taking a cigarette and placing it between his lips without lighting it. Students sometimes oohed when he did that.

"You could show these as a series," he said. "Cut them out, mat them."

Leaf said, "Maybe."

"Just a simple mat," Mr. Ware continued. He held the sketchbook to the wall and traced an imaginary border around the portrait. "Black, half-inch. That's all. With an eight-inch interval between each sketch. The viewer experiences it almost like a film." Mr. Ware moved the sketchbook along the wall, demonstrating. "See?"

"I guess."

"You guess?" Mr. Ware said. He turned to face her. "You guess that's a great idea or you guess it's a shitty one?"

Leaf felt her face grow warm.

"You know, Leaf, there's no prize for being a moody teenager. Frankly, this school is lousy with them."

"Sorry," Leaf said.

"It's a pose you might want to drop."

It's not a pose, Leaf wished to say, but didn't. She could feel herself starting to cry.

"I've really put myself out for you time and time again, in case you didn't know."

Leaf said, "I know."

Mr. Ware placed the sketchbook on his desk as if he hadn't heard. "I'm beginning to wonder if it's worth it. I really am. She's just a kid, I keep reminding myself. She doesn't know what's what. Plus I'm just some asshole to you, anyway, right? Another parent for you to act all Sylvia Plath around. Oh, tragic little me."

Leaf put her hands to her face. "I'm not trying to be tragic," she said, but she'd already begun to cry.

"You don't know what you're trying to be," Mr. Ware said.

Leaf didn't say anything. She could feel someone touching her hair, but it didn't occur to her that it must be Mr. Ware because she was crying and because it was getting dark outside and how could it be Mr. Ware? She could feel him lifting her hair from her ears and stroking it like it was something rare and impossible to touch, a lion's mane or a mermaid's locks. He did this for a few minutes while she cried. Leaf could hear him whispering, "Tragic little me," but it was like he was talking about someone else, someone they were regarding together with mild disapproval. His fingers were slow and careful. Leaf turned her head away from his touch; she couldn't bring herself to open her eyes. And it wasn't until she heard Mr. Ware walk away, heard the office door close, heard her heart beating in her ears, that she finally did.

It had gotten dark out.

The night of the open house, Leaf stood in Mr. Ware's classroom, hanging her self-portraits. She was alone, save for Alex, who had been invited to display his jumping dog painting after all, despite Mr. Ware's theatrics. Leaf watched Alex measure a white mat that was all wrong for the painting. He'd been measuring it for the past forty minutes while Leaf pretended not to notice him, even when he made little frustrated noises, or said things aloud like, "How the hell are you supposed to keep it from going *crooked*?" Leaf knew that trick: her mother used it all the time, suckering you into helping her while making it seem you'd volunteered to do so. Oh well, Leaf felt sorry for Alex. Poor Alex. So she showed him how to pick the right mat, how to align its margins just so, how to use an X-Acto to trim the inside border. Then she helped Alex hang the painting next to her portraits.

"Thanks," Alex said.

"Sure," Leaf said. The two of them stood there, looking at the painting. The dog, viewed closely, wore both an expression of joy and fear at the same time. Although his fur was childishly done—the brushstrokes all went the same direction—it drew your eye in nonetheless. You couldn't look away. Leaf said, "It's really good."

Alex laughed. "It's shit," he said.

"No, it isn't."

"You heard Ware. It's the idea of the idea or whatever."

Leaf said, "More like whatever."

Alex looked at her. "Yeah?"

"Yeah."

Alex shrugged. "If you say so." They stood that way for a few moments until Alex said, "I always thought it was pretty good, but you know, when Ware said all that crap, I kind of thought, Well, I guess he's right. And then every time I looked at it after that, I thought, Yeah, this does suck. Ware's right. You know what I mean?"

Leaf nodded.

"You do? Really?" Alex shook his head. "That's weird. I always guessed you and Mr. Ware had it all figured out. Art, I mean."

"Mr. Ware is an asshole," Leaf said.

Alex looked at her, surprised, and Leaf knew. A course of action revealed itself to her as plain and obvious as the tacks she'd used to hang her portraits. She asked Alex if he would do something for her. Alex said OK. What did she want him to do?

"Promise you'll say yes to what I'm going to ask you next," Leaf said.

"I have to promise?"

"Yes," Leaf said.

"But what if I want to say no?"

"That's what the promise is for," Leaf said.

"Oh," Alex said. He considered this. "OK, I promise."

The scissors Leaf had used all semester to cut masking tape from its heavy roll weren't nearly as sharp as the ones Mr. Ware kept in his office. The ones Leaf had sometimes played with while she sat at Mr. Ware's desk, Mr. Ware off to the teacher's lounge, letting her use his "studio" for whatever overpraised project she was working on at the time. When Leaf opened the office door with the key Mr. Ware kept hidden inside a potted fern, Alex said they shouldn't be doing this. They were going to get in trouble. And when Leaf sat at Mr. Ware's desk and handed the scissors to Alex and told him what she'd like him to do next, Alex said he wouldn't. Promise or no promise. No way. Was she crazy?

But Alex didn't back away, and, as Leaf was learning, that was agreement enough. For Alex was a good student, eager to please, and Leaf had so much to teach. And when she'd felt him close the scissors through her hair, she knew his education had begun.

NO ONE AT ALL

When Jonas was eleven, he invited Toby to the beach. Toby was thirteen, fond of hockey and tank tops. They hadn't done much together outside the neighborhood besides trick-or-treating, and didn't attend the same school. Jonas couldn't imagine hanging out with Toby at his grandfather's beach house, where you had to take a shower outdoors and sleep on a foldaway bed, always sandy, no matter how many times his mother laundered the sheets. Jonas could not imagine explaining to Toby why his mother sometimes did impromptu stretching exercises while walking the boardwalk or why his father insisted upon striping his nose with sunscreen on even the cloudiest of days. Nothing could justify his grandfather's wool bathing suit, fifty years out of style, hanging limply from the clothesline.

They spent a week in Rehoboth, the same family vacation Jonas had always known, whose chief principle seemed to be: everybody do whatever you want to do until dinnertime. Jonas and Toby spent their mornings playing video games on the rental home's television, whose picture was mysteriously cropped at the bottom with a thick black line so that, in the heat of a tank battle, it was possible to maneuver your tank into the line and fire upon your opponent from within its cloak, thrilling to Jonas, who wasn't able to beat Toby in most other things. Toby was bigger than him, stronger, less afraid. Toby could rack up four hundred points in one round of Skee-Ball, while Jonas's shots always drifted left and earned a fraction of Toby's score. Toby made small talk with concession-stand employees and had no qualms sticking his skinny arm up the throat of a vending machine to dislodge a bag of Doritos. Toby refused a prize bear on account of its pink bowtie.

These acts of self-assurance inspired two opposite feelings in Jonas: to be just like Toby and to somehow destroy him, too. He hated the way Toby walked ahead of him whenever they were out in public, but couldn't help apologizing to him for walking too slow. Jonas wanted Toby to stop calling soda "sugarwater" and pigeons "shit-birds," but introduced these words into his own speech as readily as he'd started dipping his pizza in ketchup and leaving his shoelaces untied for no reason whatsoever.

For his part, Toby seemed content to ignore Jonas for much of the day, as if Jonas were someone he'd been forced to spend time with, which was exactly the way Jonas felt about Toby, a feeling he couldn't somehow bring himself to act upon. He'd once spent an entire matinee sitting five rows behind Toby, who'd promptly left him the moment the previews began, offering no explanation. Jonas had watched the movie as if it were an elaborate backdrop to Toby's head, which reared back from time to time to accept another fistful of the popcorn Jonas had purchased for the two of them. All during the movie's predictable denouement, Jonas imagined himself telling Toby off, Toby cowering beneath Jonas's righteous rage, offering lame excuses for his thoughtlessness, excuses Jonas had no time for, ready, as he was, to point out that Toby had not *once* invited him to go anywhere, not ever; that, if it were not for him, Toby would be back in the neighborhood pedaling around on his pathetic bike; that he wasn't going to say anything but now couldn't help himself from mentioning that *both* his parents had privately commented how Toby never said anything at dinner, not even a thank-you for the time they surprised them both with ice-cream cake and sparklers. These admonishments, delivered coolly, evenly, without Jonas so much as raising his voice, would let Toby know that, no matter who he thought he was, he wasn't. He was no one, really. No one at all.

But instead of saying this, Jonas said, "You can do stuff by yourself sometimes, if you want." They were leaving the matinee, light breaking in from the exit doors. Toby tossed the empty popcorn tub into a trash barrel. "Really?" he said, without a trace of surprise.

"Yeah," Jonas said. "If you want."

Toby considered this—or was he only scouting the boardwalk for bikinis? The day before Toby had followed two girls in bikinis into a souvenir shop, Jonas in tow, mortified when Toby donned a fisherman's cap and asked the two whether they thought it made him look older. The girls had laughed.

"You can have the whole day to yourself, you know, whatever."

Toby shrugged. "I guess."

"Because it's cool with me."

Toby stopped at a photo booth and fished inside the coin return. "Fucking Canadian quarters," he said, then flung the coin over the boardwalk and onto the beach. "Did you see how far that thing went?"

"Yeah."

"Probably hit a dolphin," Toby said.

Jonas nodded, wanting to push Toby to the ground. "I think I'm going to go do some stuff," he said, experimentally. "By myself."

Toby nodded. "That dolphin is probably all like, 'Hey, what the?' "

Jonas waited for Toby to address him, but Toby only shielded his eyes, scanning the beach. "I'll see you at dinner," Jonas said.

Toby lowered his hand. "Man," he said, "this place gets so boring sometimes."

Jonas began to walk away, but Toby wasn't looking. "We're supposed to be back by five-thirty," Jonas called out. *I will keep going,* Jonas thought. *I will go quickly.* But, as Jonas fell in with the crowd moving along the boardwalk, he felt terribly alone and a second idea occurred to him: that it would be best to make Toby think he was about to leave, yet, at the same time let Toby know that he could follow him along, too, if he wanted, thereby splitting his odds and complicating Toby's choice. But, when Jonas turned to announce, "We're having barbecue chicken," Toby had already disappeared.

Jonas spent the rest of the afternoon on the boardwalk. He tried to play a few rounds of Skee-Ball, but there was no joy in it, even when he scored three-seventy-five and selected a stuffed animal snake whose eyes glowed in the dark. Toby had already won a snake just like it the day before, and had stuck the eyes to his baseball cap, which Jonas had to admit was something he'd never think of himself. It was humiliating, handing the game attendant three tokens for a game called "Steeplechase," where Jonas, despite steadily shooting water into an open bull's-eye, was unable to coax his clunky horse across the finish line, losing to a kid so young his father had to remind him to collect his prize.

All of the boardwalk's attractions were humiliating, Jonas realized, when you were alone. The whole point of the boardwalk was two of everything: two slices of pizza, two cones, two funnel cakes, two pairs of flip-flops, two T-shirts, buy one pound of saltwater taffy get the second free, two chances to shoot a basketball through a hoop barely wider than the ball itself. Walking the beach was even worse, the sand burning your feet, with no towel to return to; no one saying, "I'll watch our stuff for a while," no one to circle the other side of a sleeping sunbather you know it's going to be hilarious to talk about as soon as the two of you are out of earshot, saying, I could see *everything.* Jonas stood beneath shop awnings and browsed postcards. Jonas left a video game midway through, his doomed spaceship floating into a field of asteroids.

And yet, as soon as Jonas met up with Toby again (he found Toby rinsing his head in a public fountain) he wished to be alone. The two of them fell into step like nothing had happened outside the theater, which, in a way, it hadn't. All of Jonas's anger returned, but the speeches Jonas imagined himself delivering returned this time not with Toby's collapse, but Toby's victory. When Jonas felt himself about to say, *You know, we only have three days left here and now we've wasted this one because of your selfishness,* he now saw that Toby would say, *Well, it was your idea,* which was true and which would horribly undermine Jonas's next move, which was to say, *But I only offered because that's what I thought you wanted,* to which Toby would certainly shrug and say something like, *Well, guess you shouldn't have offered, then.*

Jonas followed Toby into a gift shop, where Toby pushed through a rack of T-shirts and crouched down before a display of rubber sharks. *Do you realize you never tell me where you're going?* Jonas wanted to say.

"These sharks are so gay," Toby said. He took one and poked his finger inside its mouth. "They're not even scary."

"Do you realize," Jonas said, "that you never tell me where you're going?"

Toby made two sharks bite each other. "Why would I?" he said.

"Because," Jonas said, "so I can know where you are."

Toby used a long stick to lift one of the sharks, whose top wore a plastic crab claw that could be opened and closed. "I'm in a store," he said.

"That's not what I mean."

"I'm in a store," Toby said. "I'm in a store and I'm bored." He crab-clawed a bag of spider rings. The rings were orange and black. "Why do they still have Halloween stuff out?"

Jonas felt his face grow warm. "I'll see you later," he said.

"Someone should tell them they still have Halloween stuff out."

Jonas pushed his way back through the T-shirts. He'd go home now. Alone. His mother was probably still reading romance novels in the rattan rocker his father had assembled the day before, his grandfather watching a ball game on TV, his father taking one of his afternoon walks to wherever it was his father took his afternoon walks to, returning, like clockwork, one half hour before dinner. He'd say hi to his mom, who'd want to know where Toby was. Jonas would shrug, saying, *Beats me.* But his mom wouldn't let him go. She'd bookmark her romance and ask him, *What happened?* and Jonas would feel his face grow warm, for he realized, pushing his way through the shop doors, that as much as he'd like to think that he could affect indifference, as much as he was sure he could keep himself from telling her what had happened, he could not disguise the blunt fact of his face, which accompanied him everywhere. His face would give him away. He'd end up telling his mother everything. He saw this as plainly as he saw tourists milling about the shop front, a space reserved for bargain items.

A cage of hermit crabs sat atop a bargain table. The crabs clung to the sides of the cage. Some of the crab's shells were painted in bright neon colors, peace symbols, or smiley faces. Jonas had seen these crabs all week—half the shops along Rehoboth Avenue sold them— but hadn't taken the time to look at them, until now. Up close, it was hard to tell if the crabs were dead or alive. A lone crab clung to the top of the cage, suspended upside down, its shell painted like the Union Jack. Jonas put his finger to the cage and touched the crab's claw. The crab released its grip and fell into a green water bowl. It lay there without moving: Jonas worried that he'd killed it. He picked up a discarded drinking straw and prodded it. The crab grabbed the straw with its surprising claw and allowed Jonas to drag it to the side of the cage.

"You gonna buy that?" an employee asked, materializing behind the cage, a teenager with a name tag and sunglasses. "Or you just want to tease him?"

Jonas told him no.

"You got money?"

Jonas said yes.

"Be sure you're not lying, because we get a lot of kids who say they're gonna buy these but don't."

Jonas sensed a few people listening to this conversation, and felt embarrassed. "I'll buy it," he found himself saying.

The teenager told him how much. Jonas handed over the money, two water-soaked dollar bills. "It's always wet," the teenager sighed, then plucked the Union Jack crab from the cage and dropped it into a Chinese food takeout box. "He's all yours, daddy."

Jonas, expecting some advice, was disappointed when the teenager took a long sip from a plastic cup and ran his hands through his hair.

"What should I feed him?" Jonas asked.

The teenager looked at him blankly. "Whatever you want to."

Jonas looked inside the container. The crab already seemed dead. "But what does he like?"

The teenager shrugged. "Who knows?"

"But what does he eat here?"

"He eats air," the teenager said, then crunched a significant chunk of ice. "Air and water and like, sand."

A moment later Toby appeared, already forgetting, it seemed, their argument inside the store. He greeted Jonas like he was pleasantly surprised to find him vacationing here, too. "What did you get?" he asked.

Jonas showed him.

"Those things die in like, three days," Toby said.

Jonas said, "Well, we'll only be here for three more days," which seemed to appease Toby. Toby took the crab from the container and placed it on his hand. The crab stuck out its claw.

"And," Toby said, "if he lives until the third day we can always kill him ourselves." For the first time that day, Toby smiled.

But the hermit crab not only lived; it seemed to thrive under Jonas's care. It would eat fish flakes, it turned out, sometimes crushed saltines, too. Jonas was pleased to discover that Toby would pay attention to him whenever they were doing something with the hermit crab, following him, even, when he allowed the crab to walk the coffee table or exchanged the old grass for new. The hermit crab also received a name: Horace.

"Horace?" Toby asked. "What kind of name is Horace?"

Jonas lifted Horace to Toby's face. "A name fur ein hermit crab, vhat else?" he said, in a rheumy, nasally voice that sometimes broke Toby up.

"Horace the Hermit Crab," Toby said.

"Das ist me," Jonas said.

Jonas tucked him inside his pocket or carried him in his hand, as the two boys went off to kill time for another day, their skin reddening in the sun. Simply adding Horace to the mix could significantly enliven nearly any activity, no matter how dull or tedious. So, another morning of tank battle took on the burnish of a cliffhanger when they placed Horace on top of the TV, where he would eventually fall off the side, signaling, in Jonas and Toby's revised rules, the end of the battle. A trip to the beach now meant something more than looking for girls with white bikinis, since Horace's life hung in the balance, Jonas and Toby taking turns tossing him into the shallow tide, then rescuing him at the last possible moment. Horace seemed to make Jonas bolder, he felt, raising him up to Toby's level. Now Jonas was no longer afraid to sit in the back section of Lou's Pizza, where kids were not supposed to go without parents, watching brave Horace walk a paper plate dusted with grated cheese. Jonas didn't mind if people noticed him cleaning Horace's shell after meals. He wasn't ashamed to give Horace a quick kiss every now and then, either. If people wanted to stare, let them, he thought, an idea as new as another Horace helped him to grasp: most people will never see you again, nor will you see them again, so it really doesn't matter what they think of you anyway. Kind Horace, helping him enlist Toby's interest, too, especially when Jonas put Horace in make-believe peril, like placing him on the trolley tracks where trolleys no longer passed, or pretended to throw him out to sea, cupping him in his hand and pocketing him all in one motion. The look on Toby's face informed Jonas that he could fool him now if he wanted to. He could do anything. He'd won. "Here," he said, permitting Toby to carry Horace home. Toby cupped him inside his palms and held him to the ocean. "See?" Toby said, in a voice Jonas didn't recognize. "That's where you used to live."

On the morning they were scheduled to leave, Jonas and Toby made their last trip to the boardwalk. It was a gray morning, threatening rain. The two boys killed time inside the arcade, spending whatever money they could beg from Jonas's parents (Toby never seemed to have his own money, another thing Jonas would have pointed out to him in their pre-Horace phase) on games they'd already grown bored of, even with Horace cheering them on. Toby's "Steeplechase" win hardly bothered Jonas; he'd already won a stuffed giraffe at "Frog Bog" that they'd abandoned inside a phone booth. They tried to make it look like the giraffe had hanged himself from the phone cord, but it just looked dumb. They put Horace inside the coin return and allowed the same quarter to fall on him, again and again, but this wasn't much fun either. Rain began to fall across the beach. Jonas always thought it was sad that the ocean got rained on, too, just like everywhere else. That didn't seem right somehow.

As they were walking back to the house, Toby said, "So how are we gonna do it?"

"Do what?"

"Kill Horace," Toby said.

Jonas couldn't remember them having ever talked about that. "I don't remember us having talked about that," he said.

Toby wiped rain from his forehead. "Flush him down the toilet is easiest," he said.

Jonas moved Horace from his hand to his pocket, where Horace forgot to retract his claw. Sometimes he forgot to retract his claw. "No," Jonas said.

"Or we could blow him up. He'd be pretty easy to blow up."

Jonas remarked that they didn't have anything to blow him up with. "Besides," Jonas said, "I'm keeping him."

Toby kicked a stone to himself. The stone was gray, mottled with black swirls. Jonas wished Toby would kick the stone to him—it would be easy enough to do—but knew he wouldn't. One time Toby solo-kicked a single acorn from the boardwalk to the house. "He wouldn't feel anything," Toby said.

"No."

"He's just going to die anyway," Toby said.

Jonas didn't say anything.

"Ka-boom," Toby said, kicking the stone. "Ka-*blooey!*"

That afternoon, they drove home. Jonas tucked Horace back into his takeout box for travel—it wasn't such a bad little carrier, really, especially with the fresh grass Jonas had added that morning, along with a few white pebbles and sand. Jonas had been serious about keeping Horace as a pet. He didn't want to give Toby the pleasure of knowing his plans, but the truth was he thought Horace could elevate him to something of a minor celebrity around the neighborhood, with Horace riding his shoulder or peeking out from his front shirt pocket. He'd never tell Toby this, but he was looking forward to keeping Horace on his nightstand, where he wouldn't be surprised to find that Horace enjoyed hearing a bedtime story or two. The thought of taking Horace to school filled Jonas with a quiet giddiness. He braced the takeout box between his feet and watched cars and station wagons passing outside, their roofs wearing flipped bicycles.

By one o'clock they were stuck in traffic. Jonas's father stared out the front window, where a moving van blocked their view. Toby put his feet to the passenger seat and played another one-player game of Head to Head Football. Jonas's mother passed around a six pack of ginger ale, bright green cans still clinging to their plastic yoke, still slightly cool, still tasting like ginger ale, a taste Jonas was just beginning to like, its slightly incorrect tartness that lingered on your tongue longer than you expected, no matter how many times you swallowed or how many potato chips you ate in between, a taste that made you feel you both craved another sip and couldn't stand another sip all at once, a taste that Jonas would forever associate with this day.

What Jonas would like to say about this day, first and foremost, is that he is sorry; he is deeply, deeply sorry. Secondly, he would like to have it known that, although he must take responsibility for what happened, and although this is something he understands completely and would not in any way wish to argue with, it nonetheless doesn't seem fair to assign blame solely on him, since he had every intention of bringing the takeout box with them *into* the Sand Dollar Diner, whose pebbled lot Jonas's father had pulled into in order to wait out the traffic, as he put it, moments before his mother said they might as well go inside and grab some lunch while they waited, an idea whose inescapable logic and common sense was as obvious and brightly lit as the blinking AIR-CONDITIONED! sign in the Sand Dollar's long window, behind which, thirty-five minutes after leaving the takeout box in the hot, window-sealed car, Jonas would find himself seated behind a grilled cheese impaled upon four feathered toothpicks; and since he was not the one who said, "Oh, going to take your *boyfriend* with you?" when he'd first lifted the takeout box from the car's floor, intending to carry it inside.

Jonas endured the longest wait he had ever known. After Jonas's mother's order arrived fifteen minutes behind everyone else's, after it took another ten minutes for ketchup to arrive, after everyone had managed to choke down their dry burgers and limp fries, Toby had asked to see the dessert menu, the waitress looking to Jonas's father for permission, Jonas's father nodding, saying, "Fine by me." Toby took his time choosing between four measly possibilities, all the while reading Jonas's thoughts, it seemed, which Jonas felt ballooning from his worried head: *I've got to check on Horace.*

Toby took three slow bites of his chocolate chip sundae before asking everyone to taste it and see if they thought it tasted funny, Jonas's mother the one to point out the obvious, that the sundae was not actually chocolate chip but *mint* chocolate chip, a flavor Toby now swore he couldn't stand, although Jonas clearly remembered the two of them polishing off a half dozen free Peppermint Patties a beach shop had unwisely left for customers in a basket near the cash register. Later, Toby went to the restroom, where it was clear he'd spent time running a wet comb through his hair, parting it neatly on the left, although he'd spent the past week walking around with a sleep-mussed cowlick so severe that even his first few dives in the ocean did nothing to flatten it. He made a *show* of holding the door for a busload of senior citizens while Jonas and his parents waited outside. He gave no look of concern when Jonas's father couldn't find his keys, the four of them baking in the sun, whose rays, Jonas glumly noticed, shone directly on the backseat, where the takeout box sat squarely in the line of fire. Toby opened his door, waved his hand in front of his face, and said, "What's that smell?"

There was no smell, Jonas would like to have it known. None whatsoever. Nothing besides the odor of a hot, beach-loaded car, where packed bathing suits still weren't completely dry and empty cans of ginger ale released their tangy breath into the air.

"Where's your *boyfriend*?" Toby laughed.

"Is that what that is?" his father said.

"No," Jonas heard himself say.

His father pulled the car out of the lot, back onto the highway, where every passenger in every passing car seemed to turn their gaze upon Jonas, who still cradled the takeout box between his feet and who would not acknowledge these people, these perfect strangers, these nobodies, whose collective gaze wished to know one thing and one thing only: *have you checked on Horace lately?*

Jonas did check on Horace, later. Only after they'd passed out of the beach communities, near the Dover Air Force Base, where cargo planes gave the false impression they were about to land on the highway, their fat bellies passing just feet above Jonas's car, where Toby took the liberty of sticking his head out the window and allowing a plane's shadow to cross his face.

Jonas opened the box. There sat Horace, dutiful Horace, doing his Horace-nothing, like always. He had his claw retracted, not unusual. He'd fallen to one side, also familiar. He looked like he always looked, Jonas thought, feeling relieved, assured, assuaged, triumphant even. He'd been foolish to be afraid. There was some kind of lesson in that, Jonas was sure. And it was only after he plucked Horace from the box and rested him on his palm that Horace's true condition revealed itself to Jonas, for Horace's claw, his wonderful, athletic claw, which had brought Jonas so many moments of joy, and which seemed to contain the very essence of Horace's personality— his fearless grasp of all that could be possibly grasped—fell onto the floor, leaving a strand of something as thin as dental floss in its wake.

In a moment Toby would ask him what was that? What fell? And Jonas would feel tears forming, tears he wouldn't be able to hold back. The tears that would embarrass him forever, making it impossible to ever hang out with Toby again. He'd wipe the tears away, his mother turning and asking what's wrong, honey? His father would slow the car to the side of the road, where Jonas would cry for longer than he'd ever cried before, a baby. That's what he'd be in a moment: a baby. He'd put his head to his knees, feel his mother's hand upon his shoulder. He'd make whimpering noises.

None of that happened before another plane passed overhead. Toby stuck his head out the window, the wind taking his hair. "It's like it's going to land on us," Toby said. A shadow lengthened across the car. A roar descended, like a sustained thunderclap. Jonas looked at Toby and saw the shadow swallow him whole.

"We're dead," Toby said. "Dead, for real dead."

AFTER THE FINALE

The grandfather doesn't want to take the grandchildren to see the fireworks, but they keep begging him, and he ends up giving in, the way he always does. When will he stop giving in? The grandchildren pile into the grandfather's Jeep, which exudes the smell of damp tools. The grandchildren neglect seat belts. They flip the tops of the ashtrays and roll the windows up and down. "Drive fast," they say, "or we'll miss everything." They are ugly grandchildren. The grandfather doesn't keep a picture.

The drive takes longer than it should. When they arrive at the stadium parking lot, the fireworks are already ending. A furious sky of red and pink blooms across the windshield.

"It's the finale," the grandfather tells them.

"It's not the finale," one grandchild says, the one who has a habit of rolling his nose pickings into little pills. He kicks the grandfather's seat.

"Yeah, it's not," the other grandchild says, the one whose sneakers can mutate into roller skates.

The grandfather rolls his window down. This is the stadium he used to come to as a kid, with his dad, his father sometimes letting him drink a beer on the sly. The air is thick with sulfur. Between explosions, the grandfather can hear the closing measures of the *1812 Overture*. People clap and whistle. The show ends.

"We missed it," Pills sighs.

"The Fourth of July," Sneakers says. His voice verges on tears.

The grandfather turns to face them. "'Least we saw a little," he says, resenting the false cheer in his voice. Why is he always wishing to act cheery? That evening, he'd let the grandchildren eat raspberry sherbet straight out of the carton.

"You didn't drive fast enough," Pills says.

"You're a slowpoke," Sneakers explains.

Sometimes, after the ball game, his father would take him to a bar near the stadium. The Extra Inning. His father would let him sit on a barstool and order him as many Roy Rogers as he wanted while his father played pool under the smoky pool lamp, whose glass shade showed a salmon leaping from a waterfall. He'd drink Roy Rogers after sickly sweet Roy Rogers, which the bartender, Squinny, had fitted out with an extra maraschino cherry, just for him. Maraschino cherries were the best part about a Roy Rogers.

"We didn't even see the *whole* finale," Pills says, but the grandfather doesn't say anything. Instead he pulls the Jeep out of the stadium parking lot, where traffic is already bumper-to-bumper. They ride behind a pickup truck with five teens juddering in the back. An SUV tails him, honks when the grandfather allows a station wagon to pull ahead.

"We'll never get home," Pills sighs.

"There is no home for us anymore," Sneakers says in a dramatic British accent, which cracks the two of them up. "We shan't be going home at all," they laugh. "We simply *shan't*."

One night, at The Extra Inning, a woman had sat next to the grandfather, a friend, his father explained. Darla. She'd sat with the two of them while his father waited for his turn at pool. She wore a green dress and stirred her drink with a tiny plastic stick. She asked the grandfather questions about school, about girls he liked. *Tiger,* she kept calling him. She'd had to lean into him to hear his embarrassed answers, affording a sudden glimpse of her bra, just visible beneath the neckline of her dress. He'd felt her breath against his cheek. *Tiger.* From time to time his father would stop by, give him a little punch on the shoulder. "She sweet talkin' you?" his father would say, then line up his next shot. Whenever his father lined up a shot, he always measured the angle with the tip of his cue. He'd crouch down, measuring, then chalk the cue like it was something he was trying to ignite.

Now, the grandfather catches a glimpse of the stadium in his rearview mirror, a fantastic, flipped chandelier. The grandchildren press their faces to the windows. "Ah see mahself," Sneakers says. Pills laughs. "Me, too." They kiss the glass, giggle. The grandfather thinks about telling them to stop, but doesn't. This is his second night in a row looking after the grandchildren while their mother goes on a date with a man she met at a bowling alley. Since his daughter's divorce, the grandfather has been watching the grandkids when she can't find a sitter, or won't pay for one. "Do you know how much they get nowadays?" she'd asked him, spooning macaroni and cheese onto the grandchildren's plates. He'd guessed low, to please her. "Jesus, Dad," she'd sighed, "who'd do *anything* for that?"

The night Darla sat next to him, the grandfather watched his father lose to a local, a man everyone called Farmer. Farmer wore the thickest glasses the grandfather had ever seen, which caught the light from the pool lamp, and slid down his nose whenever he'd completed his shot. Farmer never spoke, never watched his opponent's shot, a technique that maddened his father to the point that he would take foolish shots, try unlikely combinations, commit rookie errors. Afterward, he'd sat next to Darla and put his elbows to the bar, while Squinny drew him a Pabst Blue Ribbon. Darla said things the grandfather couldn't hear. She described tiny circles on his father's back. The grandfather felt his face grow warm. "Hey," his father said, after a few beers, "you wanna see Darla do a little trick?"

"I'm not doing the trick, Frank," Darla said.

"The little one," his father said. "Do the little trick."

"Not the little trick."

"Aw, the kid will love it," his father said. "Tell her you'll love it."

"I'll love it," the grandfather said, dutifully. Darla looked at him like someone she felt sorry for, and then pointed to his Roy Rogers. "I'll need a cherry."

"Give her a cherry," his father said. The grandfather complied.

"I haven't done this in a while," Darla said, sticking the cherry in her mouth, "so it might not come out right." She held up a finger, as if to say *wait,* and chewed the cherry for what seemed too long a time.

"You'll love this," his father said.

Darla moved her tongue inside her cheeks, covered her mouth with one hand, and then extended her tongue, where the cherry stem lay tied into a knot. "Ta-da," she said.

"Wow," the grandfather said. The stem was tightly tied.

His father gave him a look he would not forget, a look around which all of these other memories—Darla, Squinny, Farmer, the Roy Rogers, the pool lamp—gloomily lingered. "Isn't that something?" his father said.

* * *

By the time they arrive home, the grandchildren have fallen asleep. The grandfather must carry Sneakers, while Pills wakes up enough to climb upstairs and crawl into bed without changing out of his clothes. They sleep in the guest bedroom, two to a bed, where a sewing dummy presides. The grandfather has been meaning to get rid of the dummy since his wife died, but has never gotten around to it. He knows he never will, the way he's starting to know things like that now. The dummy's head still wears the eyelashes his daughter inked when she was a kid. Downstairs, he hears her return. Keys tossed onto the kitchen table. A beer unburdened of its cap.

"Did you get their shoes?" the daughter asks, when the grandfather enters the kitchen.

He tells her he did. "But I wasn't sure about the socks."

"Socks are nothing," she says. "Don't worry about socks." They sit at the table and drink beer, although the grandfather knows he shouldn't drink so late at night. He's going to regret it, he can tell, as he is not asking his daughter about her date, but what should he ask?

"All my life, I've been happiest in a kitchen," she says, after a while. "Even when I was little. Sometimes I used to sneak downstairs when you and Mom were sleeping, just to sit in the kitchen. I wouldn't even fix a snack. I was never hungry. I'd just sit at the table for a few minutes and really get into the idea of being in the kitchen, you know?" She takes a sip of beer. "Then I'd feel dumb and sneak back upstairs."

"Hmm," the grandfather says, not wanting to contradict his daughter's version of herself, which, in most of her recollections, seems to be of a solitary girl, horribly alone and isolated, far removed from the one he remembers hosting sleepovers and starring in school musicals. "We never knew."

"I always hoped you'd find me sitting there," she says. "Like you'd come in and be amazed or angry or confused or whatever you'd be."

"Not angry," the grandfather says, sensing this is the wrong tack. Outside, the grandfather can hear a few fireworks, probably neighbors shooting bottle rockets. He wonders if he should wake the grandkids.

"One time I sat here for a really long time. It was probably only twenty minutes or something, but it felt like hours. I kept thinking you were about to come in. Like it was going to happen any minute, but it didn't. Nothing happened. I sat in the kitchen and listened to the clock tick. After a while, I turned off the lights and went upstairs."

Don't say sorry, the grandfather thinks. Outside, another firework, this one louder, closer.

"But, know what? Before I went to bed I stopped in front of your door. Remember the way you and Mom always kept the door propped open with that funny little doorstop, that little poodle thing?"

"Beagle."

"Right—the beagle! Anyway, I remember looking into your room, but not really wanting to look into it, either. I remember reaching down and moving the beagle. Couldn't believe how heavy it was."

"How heavy it was," the grandfather says.

"And the door just slammed—wham! I had no idea it would slam," she says, takes a long sip of beer. "I ran to my room as fast as I could."

"So that was you?" the grandfather says, chancing a joke, but his daughter looks at him in a way that lets him know he's disappointed her. Again. When will he stop disappointing his daughter? They drink another beer, make small talk for a while, until his daughter announces she's going to bed.

"Goodnight," the grandfather says.

"Goodnight."

The grandfather decides he should rinse their empty bottles, but finds himself unable to leave the kitchen table. Like his daughter. He can understand why she snuck downstairs as a kid, why she hoped someone would discover her. And, because he understands, he knows he will never tell her that her memory of the slammed door is incorrect. For he hadn't been asleep when she pulled the beagle away; he'd been looking right at her. He'd seen her. And he'd always thought she'd seen him, too, as the door closed not with a slam, but with a slow sigh, the doorway a narrowing aperture that diminished and diminished until he could no longer see her and she could no longer see him.

THE NATURE AND AIM OF FICTION

The year before Katherine went to college, Colin picked her up to take her to his creative writing class. Colin was her boyfriend, eighteen years old to Katherine's seventeen, Katherine still a high school senior, still a semester away from graduating, still needing her parents' permission to visit Colin's campus. They'd been dating for five months. Colin was wearing his favorite cardigan, too hot even for October. Katherine had helped him pick it out a few weeks ago at the thrift store. Colin had stood before the store's lone mirror, appraising himself, as Katherine looked on. He'd asked her what she thought. Katherine told him he looked good. No, Colin had said, he wanted to know what she really thought. What she really thought, Katherine said, was that he looked good in that cardigan. He should buy it. There had been a moment when Colin raised his jaw to the mirror and asked, But doesn't it make me look like a young old man? when Katherine had glimpsed something ugly and vaguely menacing about Colin, something she had always sort of known about him, without quite knowing what it was really.

They hadn't even left the parking lot before Colin began explaining how the creative writing class worked. The class was not a lecture or seminar, as most of Katherine's high school classes were; this was a college workshop, an altogether different animal, Colin assured her. In a writing workshop, students sat with the teacher at a long table, so that thoughts and ideas and suggestions might flow freely. Even, Colin wasn't too shy to admit, a little bit of praise, from time to time, of course.

"How do you all fit at one table?" Katherine asked.

Colin ignored her. "We are a small group," he said, "but a group committed to treating each and every word as if it were a rare gem." This sounded like something Colin's teacher had said to him or something he'd read somewhere or a hearty combination of both.

Katherine said, "But how does everyone sit together at one table?"

Colin sighed. "It's actually four tables shoved together."

"Oh."

"I don't see why you are so fascinated by the table."

"I was just trying to picture it," Katherine said. "Sorry."

The year before, Colin had given Katherine a ride home from band practice. A ride that led, in Katherine's backward remembrance, to mini golf to a movie to late night phone calls in her parents' laundry room, where Katherine was able to drag their ancient landline phone, whose receiver gave off a faint smell of sweat and Windex. The feel of the heavy phone against her ear and Colin's deep voice and the crisp, tart scent of ammonia all caught up in Katherine's sense of *falling in love,* although she was glad no one knew she thought so. Especially Colin, who, in the weeks leading up to sex, had gotten Katherine to agree that *falling in love* was a meaningless phrase, too common and mainstream for them. They would be wise, Colin convinced her, to sidestep it altogether. Katherine had nodded, as she lowered Colin's boxers to his ankles.

"You know," Colin said, "I only asked you to come with me today because I thought you might like to see what a real college class is like, but now I feel like I've forced you into going. If you want, I can drop you off at the library. I don't want you to feel any sense of—" Colin searched for just the right gems, "undue obligation."

Katherine told him that she wanted to go. She was looking forward to it, she said.

"Well," Colin said, "if you're looking forward to it. But I do think you'd enjoy the library."

"Colin, I don't want to go to the library. I want to go to your class."

"They have an excellent selection of bound journals, and the café, although limited in its offerings, can at least claim a refreshing lack of pretention."

"Colin, don't be ridiculous! I want to come to class with you. This means a lot to me, OK?" Katherine was careful not to say, *It means a lot to me that you asked me.* Since relinquishing her virginity, she was trying to be careful about saying things like that. "I can't wait to see a real college class."

Colin said, "Well, if you really want to."

They drove the rest of the way with Colin explaining the workshop process to her. The class would invite him to read a selection from his story aloud, perhaps a page or two, and then Colin was to assume a respectful silence for the rest of his workshop, free to take notes, but not to interject, object, or comment on the discussion of his story, since doing so would violate the workshop's sacred creed, namely that it was the text the class was there to talk about, not the writer. The text was everything; the writer and the writer's intentions meant nothing. The text was God.

"The text?" Katherine asked. "You mean, the 'story'?"

"Yes."

"Why don't you just say the 'story,' then?"

"Because doing so would accidentally confirm that we agree, prior to discussing the text, that the text is in fact a story, when our discussion might lead us to conclude the opposite."

"Oh," Katherine said. She looked out the window, where the campus was beginning to insist upon itself. "But it's a short story class, right? I mean, how could it not be a story?"

Colin laughed. "To this question," he said, "our discussion must surely rise."

The weekend they'd first had sex was the weekend Colin had given Katherine his short story "These Are Not Your Hands." They'd returned to Colin's dorm to find Colin's roommate gone, a rare occurrence, as unusual as Colin washing his sheets, which gave off the odor of damp rocks as Colin moved inexpertly above Katherine, his expression strangely fearful, as if Katherine was someone who, in fact, terrified him. He'd finished too quickly, and apologized, and Katherine knew it was her duty to console him. First sex, an embarrassing thing, Katherine would later think. Painful, too. Colin a starter boyfriend, Katherine's next year would have her know, something she had to go through, to endure, to survive; some vague yet terribly important passage whose meaning was still up for grabs. Katherine would spend months trying to figure it out. Years.

Katherine had read the story right after Colin dropped her back home, beneath the nimbus of light from her embarrassing Snoopy desk lamp. The story began with a young boy waking up in a house where everyone seems to have vanished. If the boy finds this strange, he draws no attention to it; instead he wanders around the house, minutely observing, for reasons that aren't quite clear, a thunderstorm that seems to be moving in, its clouds "dark and even darker and full of shadow." The boy walks to the bathroom, where he observes himself in the mirror above the sink for nearly four pages, although nothing really happens there, aside from the boy noting that the lines on his hands and the pattern of the floor tile are both "cruciform." He drinks a glass of water, but not before raising it above his head, "in the manner of a priest," and sets it back down upon the sink, whose faucet is "T-shaped."

Next, the boy peeks into his parents' bedroom. His mother is asleep, her slumbering body crisscrossed by the rays of morning light coming from the bedroom window, also cruciform, the sun "like their father's presence among them," although we don't know where the father is, or, Katherine noted, how beams of anything could come through that thunderstorm on page one. The boy sits next to his mother, noting the wrinkles in her hands. He puts his hand in hers so that the lines of their hands might join in "an unspoken harmony," and then picks up an empty whiskey bottle and carries it to the bathroom. He studies himself in the mirror again when he dumps the whiskey into the sink (wait, wasn't it empty?) where, for reasons more cryptic than twice studying oneself in a bathroom mirror in just under six pages, the boy places both hands to the glass and whispers, "These are not your hands."

Downstairs, the boy finds a birthday cake sitting on the kitchen table. The boy draws near, his heart beating as he rises up on tiptoes to read the lettering on the top: HAPPY BIRTHDAY, SCOTTIE. The boy turns the cake toward him and sits at the table. He drags his finger through the icing and licks it with his tongue. "They got my name wrong," the boy sighs, "my name isn't Scottie, it's Jimmy." His disappointment aside, Jimmy places a birthday hat upon his head and blows halfheartedly though a plastic whistle that "refuses to sound."

Jimmy is jolted from his reverie when the thunderstorm, newly remembered and very much resembling a category five hurricane, sends the lights flickering on Jimmy's solo birthday bash. Jimmy, quietly singing "Happy Birthday" to himself now, is startled by a thunderclap that accompanies the sudden opening of the kitchen door, hitherto unmentioned, like the man standing in its frame, lightning crashing behind him. "What you doing, boy?" he bellows. Jimmy doesn't say anything. "You having yourself a little birthday party?" Jimmy looks up at the man, who, we are later informed in a long monologue delivered while the man hangs up his raincoat, is Jimmy's stepfather, Devlin. Devlin, his breath reeking of whiskey and his clothes exuding "the aroma that is the aroma of cheap prostitutes all across the globe," sits down at the table and begins drinking from a flask.

Jimmy, lost in yet another reverie about time and memory, studies the lines of the cake, which command his complete attention, despite the storm tearing the roof off the house, which is now "doused in darkness." In the dark, Jimmy and Devlin inexplicably begin singing "Happy Birthday" together, although rain is now pouring in from two cracks in the ceiling, also cruciform, and also extinguishing the birthday candles on Jimmy's cake, which Katherine couldn't recall anyone lighting? Next, a thunderclap shakes the entire house, ending Jimmy and Devlin's song. Devlin is about to raise his whiskey flask to his lips, when Jimmy brings his hands down—splat!—through the center of the cake. The two of them stare at Jimmy's hands, which have left a curious shape in the icing. The story ends with Jimmy licking the icing from his hands, hands that seem suddenly strange to him, like nothing he's ever known.

Katherine read the story a second time, to see if it was as bad as she thought it was, but her second reading only wished to confuse her first impression, which, her second reading would have her know, was too eager to find fault with what wasn't good while passing over what actually was. Like Jimmy's loneliness, which Colin had done a fine job capturing, or the scene in the mother's bedroom, which Katherine saw as clearly and plainly as if she were witnessing it firsthand. She could see the wetness clinging to the whiskey bottle's bottom. The faint circle the bottle left upon the nightstand. The story was both bad and good and good and bad, often simultaneously, the second reading revealed, although how such a thing was possible, Katherine did not understand. She fell asleep trying. Years later, whenever a boyfriend asked Katherine about her first boyfriend, Katherine would laugh and tell them about Colin, about the day he took her to his writing workshop, about their awkward and embarrassing sex, about Colin's short story. About their breakup.

Sounds like a real jerk, the boyfriend would say.

Oh, I guess he was, Katherine would say, and he wasn't.

* * *

Colin led Katherine across campus to the English department, where Colin's class was held in a room little different from the ones at Katherine's high school, save for the large table at the center, composed, as Colin had correctly stated, of four rectangular tables. They arrived early and took seats farthest from the head of the table. A green chalkboard held the ghosts of dead scribbles; Katherine tried to make them out, these runes, these hieroglyphs to college discourse, but the only words she could discern were "do" and "not" and "erase." There were only a handful of students there, two of whom said hello to Colin when he walked in. A guy in a backward baseball cap told Colin he thought his story was totally cool. "Thanks, Jason," Colin said, but didn't introduce Katherine, even when Colin sat down next to him, leaving no room for Katherine.

"You can get one of those chairs," Colin said, indicating a stack of plastic chairs shoved against the opposite wall. Katherine dragged one over, but not before apologizing to a girl she nearly knocked into, a girl dressed in dark jeans, a glossy black belt, black Doc Martens, and a white T-shirt decorated with what looked like a furious ink sketch of Wilma Flintstone and Betty Rubble. Her skin was pale, but pretty, her face void of makeup.

"Sorry," Katherine said. Not Wilma and Betty, she thought, but so recognizable. Who?

"Whatever," the girl said. She made a quiet snorting sound and took a seat at the opposite corner from Colin. Katherine sat next to him and waited for Colin to introduce her to everyone, but Colin only took out a notebook and opened it to a blank page. "HANDS" he wrote at the top.

After a few more students trickled in, the professor appeared, late, but clutching a steaming mug of coffee, whose side bore the call letters of the local NPR station. In his other hand he held a thick sheaf of papers, which he threw onto the table with a theatrical flourish. "That," he announced, "is what a stillborn novel looks like, my friends."

The class broke into nervous laughter, but if this was the reaction the professor intended, it was hard to say. He was about fifty, Katherine figured, with thinning hair and tortoiseshell glasses, which he wiped against his brown bomber jacket, too short in the sleeves, its zipper separating from the fabric. His skin was mottled and raw-looking, his teeth bad. He offered them a clumsy smile and said, "So much for nine years of labor, eh?"

The class reeled. Nine years! No! they said. Not nine years!

"Yes," the professor said, "I'm afraid so." He chuckled, even though Colin had told Katherine he forbade anyone to use that word in their stories. "But we've parted company amicably, this old stillborn novel and I, me a little wiser perhaps, and the world of letters as indifferent as it was before I set sail." He looked around the room, but if he registered Katherine's strange presence among the other students, he made no indication of it. "But, behold it, students, for a failed piece of writing is there to remind us that bad writing often takes as long as good writing, longer even, I'd say, as much as we'd like to believe it wasn't so. It is so, these dead pages wish to say. It is so."

There followed a ten-minute discussion about the creative process, wherein Colin mentioned that even Stephen King had tossed *Carrie* into the wastebasket before his wife retrieved it and sent it to a publisher.

"Which we won't hold against her for the moment," the professor joked.

No, Colin said, he only wanted to mention that despair was part of the writing process.

"The largest part," the professor laughed. He spent the next few minutes reading aloud from the novel, which sounded pretty good to Katherine, although the professor kept stopping to annotate each section with a self-deprecating observation. The class, Colin included, loved this. They smiled at one another, laughed. They ate it up.

Except for the girl with the strange T-shirt, Katherine noticed. She stared at her fingers, which each wore a tiny black ring.

After the professor had read another few hilariously bad-but-good pages, he checked his watch and said, "Well, I suppose we could just do a writing exercise today and leave a bit early."

"We've got a story today, professor," Jason said.

"Yeah, we have Colin's story," the girl with the T-shirt said. Her voice was accusatory; the entire class turned to look at her. Colin, Katherine noted, was quietly beaming.

"Oh, Colin's story, of course," the professor said. He began rifling through his papers. "Sorry about that, Colin." He reached under the desk and produced a leather satchel as wrinkled and beaten as his bomber jacket. "I hadn't forgotten. Just had my days mixed up, is all." He pulled out a stack of papers bound by rubber bands. "It's in this one, I know it." He removed the rubber band, which snapped between his fingers. "I know I put it in here last night. I distinctly remember putting it in here last night. Listen, why don't we just have Colin read a bit to us, and we'll all get started while I find my copy. Sound good? And thanks to Daphne for keeping this absentminded professor from dementia's abyss for at least another hour."

Daphne declined to return the professor's smile. She produced an exotic pen the size of a peacock's feather and began doodling in her notebook. Colin took out his manuscript, as did the other students. He began to read. He read from the section with Jimmy and his mother in the bedroom. Katherine listened as Colin got to the part where Jimmy picked up the whiskey bottle. Colin's voice was measured and slow, confident, but without his usual arrogance. He was a good reader. His voice guided Katherine deeper into the story than she'd been before. Like how she didn't notice the moment when Jimmy moved a comma of hair behind his mother's ear, the hair curling beneath her chin. That was a good moment. Katherine could see Jimmy doing that.

"Thank you, Colin," the professor said. Colin nodded. The professor said, "Who would like to begin?"

For a moment that seemed longer than it needed to be, no one said a word. Students eyed each other noncommittally. A car passed outside. After it had gone, a guy in an Army jacket said, "I wondered about the cross imagery."

Another girl said, "Yeah, I agree with Nick; that was weird. I mean, at first I thought it was really cool, you know? Like the way he keeps seeing crosses everywhere? I really liked that, but then I was like, Wait, why does he keep seeing crosses everywhere? I thought that was kind of confusing." The girl flipped through her manuscript, reliving her confusion. Other students nodded. Katherine heard a few whisper, "Yeah, me too." The girl continued, "I guess what I mean is that I really thought it was cool except for how I had no idea what was going on." She looked at the professor, who was reading the manuscript, newly found, with what seemed strange gravity. "I mean, I think I kind of resisted that?"

"Yeah, I agree with Eliza," a girl wearing a purple headband said. "I was all into this little kid walking around this house, but then he started seeing crosses everywhere, and I was so confused. I was like, 'What is he doing? Why is he smashing a birthday cake?' I had no idea what was going on."

"But that's the best part!" Jason said. "You're not *supposed* to have any idea what's going on. That's the whole *point*. Because this kid has no idea what's going on, and so neither do you." Katherine could see Colin beginning to smile. "I mean," he continued, "I liked how I had no idea what was going on." He looked over at Colin the way Colin had mentioned they weren't supposed to, the writer dead to the discussion, obsolete, unseen. "I thought you could even make it *more* confusing," he said. "You know? Just make it like he has no idea what the hell is going on?" Katherine watched Colin jot down "add confusion."

The professor, turning to the last page of the manuscript, said, "You want it more confusing, Jason?"

"Yeah," Jason said.

"You like being confused?"

"Yeah. It's awesome. Have you ever seen that movie *Memento*?"

"Oh my God," the girl in the headband said. "That movie was so weird!" The class began to discuss how weird *Memento* was, but the professor waved his hands and interrupted them. "Well, Jason," he said, "I have some very interesting news for you; I have just decided on your final grade." He opened his roll book and scribbled something down.

"Awesome," Jason said.

"Would you like to know what it is?"

"You bet."

"Your final grade is an asterisk and half an ampersand," the professor said.

"Is that like an A?"

"I don't know," the professor admitted. "But it *is* very confusing and I'm sure you'll enjoy it."

After the class had finished laughing, the professor steered them back to Colin's story, which, he said, did a fine job creating a feeling of unease in the reader. That was true, Katherine thought; it did create a feeling of unease.

"But it doesn't make any sense," a guy in a long-sleeved T-shirt said. "I see what Nick and Megan are saying, but I just thought this little kid was a total whiner, you know? If he was my kid, I'd be like, 'Stop sticking your goddamn hands all over my house, you little brat!'"

"I agree with what Brian just said," Megan said. "I resisted Jimmy sticking his hands all over everything."

"I also resisted that," a girl with a note on her hand said. *Get $$,* the note read. "And why did he go into his mother's bedroom? I didn't get that either."

"Because she's sleeping," Jason said. "He's thinking about waking her up."

"So he just wanders into his mother's bedroom and starts playing with her hair?" the girl with the note said. "Who would do that?"

"Duh, Laura, he's a little kid," Jason said.

"Right," Laura said, "so why does he spend half the story staring into the mirror thinking about—" she flipped through the manuscript, "'time's great arrow arching across an unknown sky'?"

"I resisted the unknown sky," another girl said, her skin tanned the color of a ripe clementine.

"No little kid stares into mirrors thinking about time's great arrow or whatever," Laura said. "Little kids are into video games and TV and stuff."

"Isn't that a generalization?" someone asked. The class looked to the professor, as if for confirmation, but before he could answer, Daphne said, "This story is perfect. Don't change one word." She was still scribbling something with her odd pen, this time directly onto Colin's manuscript, which looked, even from a distance, significantly read and reread. She spoke without looking up. Colin's face held a look of barely restrained jubilation. Katherine felt the air slowly shutting off around her.

"Would anyone like to address Daphne's assertion?" the professor asked. Before anyone could answer, he asked, "Can we ever truly proclaim a workshop story finished? Or," he said, giving the class a sly smile, "is this a rigged game, a marked deck?"

"I think a workshop story can be finished," Laura said, "but I just don't think the kid in this story would do the things he does, that's all."

"A question of motivation," the professor said.

"Like," Laura continued, "why would he look into the mirror and think about his father while his mom is passed out in the bed like a drunk zombie? Why would anyone do that?"

Daphne drew something dramatic across Colin's manuscript and said, "Father, son, and Holy Spirit."

When she said that, Colin's lips gave way to a smile Katherine had never seen before, a smile that showed all of his not-terribly-straight teeth, and strung sudden wrinkles from the corners of his eyes. His face reddened. He wrote "THANK YOU!" in his notebook and drew thick lines radiating to the edge of the page.

"What do you mean, father, son, and Holy Spirit?" Megan said.

"The Holy Trinity," Daphne said. She did not look up.

"Is that a symbol or something?" Jason said.

"How is the mother the Holy Spirit?" Laura said.

"Maybe she's a symbol," Jason offered.

"Yeah, a drunk one," Laura said.

A discussion of the use of symbols in literature followed, something Katherine would have normally enjoyed, but not today. For she was watching Daphne as Jason, Laura, and Megan argued whether the writer should put symbols in a story (Jason: That's the whole *point!* Laura: The point of what? Jason: Of *writing!* Laura: The point of writing is to put a lot of symbols in? Jason: So the reader can find them and be like, holy shit, that's *deep!*) or whether a story would be better not using symbols at all (Laura: Sign me up. Megan: Maybe you could just sprinkle a few in for fun? Professor: Even though all language is, at root, symbolic). Daphne was drawing again, now sitting in such a way that Katherine could stare at her T-shirt, which was not an ink sketch of Wilma Flintstone and Betty Rubble after all; it was an ink sketch of Frida Kahlo and Madonna. Together. A thought balloon floated squiggly above their ink heads. "Is it?" the balloon read.

The class finished talking about symbols and gave Colin some line edits. Colin nodded and marked these on his manuscript, but not, Katherine noted, with a pen; he'd chosen a pencil for this task, his edits so faint they bordered on invisibility. Conversation faltered.

Katherine wondered why no one had acknowledged her presence in class today. That seemed odd to Katherine. If someone visited her school, the teacher would always introduce them, no matter what. Maybe it was another college thing Katherine didn't understand, not introducing class visitors, that and the way Daphne had acted toward the professor—if she pulled that kind of attitude she'd get a demerit, or even be sent to the office. Why did Daphne think Colin's story was perfect? Did she really think so?

The professor gave some closing remarks about the importance of storytelling, something every writer was at great pains to keep in mind each time he or she launched off on a journey across the blank page, for a writer's job was not to show how intelligent he or she was, how well read, how clever, how funny, or how sensitive; a writer's job was to tell the reader a story, period. "And you are one intelligent, well-read, clever, funny, and sensitive writer, Colin," the professor said. "The next step is to find the story."

Colin nodded.

"And now, Colin, you may ask the class some questions, if you like. But please—" the professor held off and allowed the class to finish the sentence for him. "No rebuttals!" the class laughingly chorused. Colin smiled and made a pretense of jotting something on his manuscript, although only Katherine saw he wasn't writing anything at all. After a moment passed, in which Colin had authored the longest faux note Katherine had ever witnessed, he set his pencil down and said, "I appreciate all of your comments, edits, and suggestions. Certainly they will help guide me as I enter the revision process."

The class pounded Colin with questions. What was up with all the crosses? Were they symbols? Were his hands symbols? Was Daphne right? Was the bedroom scene a symbol of the Holy Trinity? What did the thunderstorm symbolize? Was Devlin the devil? Why did Jimmy's name begin with J?

Colin shrugged. "I leave those questions to the reader," he said, but couldn't disguise the smile now forming across his face, the one that would part the moment he said what he was going to say next, which was, "But I will admit that it will be hard for me to revise any of this, because all of it is true."

Katherine looked to the professor, who was nodding as if he suspected as much. Was no one in the class going to ask how Colin had survived a hurricane while standing up to his drunken stepfather? What about smashing the cake? Katherine couldn't recall Colin mentioning any of these events to her, let alone an alcoholic mother and departed father. The one time Katherine had met Colin's father, he hadn't given off the least whiff of dead. Katherine watched a few students forming some of these questions themselves, but there was one student who was doing something none of them were. From the opposite end of the table, Daphne was clapping. Applauding. The class turned to her.

"Don't change one word," she said. Her stare, aimed at Colin, froze the class nonetheless, who had started to gather up their belongings before Daphne started clapping. They looked to Colin, as if asking permission to depart. Colin bowed and whispered, "Thank you. That's very kind." When Katherine looked over to him, she could see that he was trembling. She was about to congratulate him on his workshop, when Colin hurriedly stuffed all of his manuscripts (the class had returned their edited copies to him) into his book bag, stood from the table, and walked quickly to the door.

"Colin," Katherine said. She followed him into the hallway, where he was already heading through an exit when she yelled, "Colin! Wait up!" and he turned to look at her with an expression that conveyed genuine surprise at finding her here today, in this hallway, on campus, right when he was leaving class. "Colin, what are you doing?" Katherine said. "Why did you leave me in there?"

Colin urged her outside, where he took shelter under a collegial oak and said, "Did you hear them in there? God! The din of an angry mob." He snorted. "They really read me the riot act, didn't they?" He shook his head. "So this is what it feels like to be tarred and feathered."

Tarred and feathered? "I thought they really liked it," Katherine said.

"They were trying to be nice," Colin said. "That's their idea of kindness, thinly veiled cruelty."

"But your professor said you were intelligent and sensitive."

"Intelligent and sensitive, oh great!" Colin spat. "That's just great, isn't it? Just what the world needs, another intelligent and sensitive hack with aspirations. A dime a freaking dozen, I'd say."

Katherine didn't know what to say. She could see that Colin was upset, and that any counterargument to his feelings would only upset him further, so she put her arms around him, but Colin pushed her away. "The whole thing was a sham," he said. "A parade of false praise and lies. God, you could hear it in everyone's voice, they just wanted to rip it apart, tear it to its amateurish shreds."

Katherine was going to say how much Daphne seemed to like it, but two things prevented her from saying so: one; she discovered she couldn't bear to say that girl's name, and two, Daphne had just materialized beside them, unlocking her bike from a rack shaped like a Slinky.

"Hey," Daphne said.

"Hey, Daphne," Colin said.

Daphne approached them. She was holding the largest bike lock Katherine had ever seen, a long chain painted bright gold with hot pink sparkles. When Daphne spoke next, she placed the lock around her neck as casually as one might a winter scarf. "Don't listen to them, Colin," she said. "I'm serious. That whole class is a crock of shit. I can hardly stand any of them anymore."

Katherine was rehearsing what she'd say when Colin introduced them, when Colin said, "It does seem like a racket, doesn't it?"

"Biggest dog and pony show in town," Daphne said. "Creative writing in academia."

Colin laughed. "An indicting accusation."

"I like your shirt," Katherine said. "Is that Frida Kahlo and Madonna?"

"Is it?" Daphne said, echoing the shirt's provocation.

"I don't know, is it?" Katherine asked.

"Is it?" Daphne said. She smiled, revealing her pretty teeth. Daphne was kind of pretty, Katherine realized, and felt something fold within her chest.

"Daphne is a studio art major," Colin said, as if to explain Daphne's behavior.

"Oh," Katherine said.

"Am I?" Daphne laughed.

"She is," Colin said. "And a super-talented one."

"Well, I really like your shirt," Katherine said. "Madonna and Frida Kahlo. That would be a really cool conversation, I mean, if they could be together."

"Would it?" Daphne said. She sat astride her bike, which was festooned with eyes cut from magazines.

"Yeah," Katherine said.

"Daphne doesn't like to discuss her work," Colin said.

"Don't I?" Daphne said.

"Oh," Katherine said. "Sorry."

"Are you?" Daphne said, but before Katherine could say anything, both Daphne and Colin burst out laughing. Colin gave Daphne what seemed to Katherine a conspiratorial look.

"Well, it was nice meeting you," Katherine said, and immediately wanted to throw herself off a cliff.

"Is it?" Daphne said. She gave them each a salute and began pedaling away. "It is!" she called out as she hopped a curb and cut between two students tossing a yellow Frisbee. "Madonna and Kahlo!"

When they were back in Colin's dorm room, Katherine said, "Why didn't you tell me about Daphne?" They were sitting on his narrow bed. Colin had his hands beneath Katherine's shirt.

"What do you mean?"

"I mean why didn't you tell me about Daphne, that's what."

Colin removed his hands from her breasts. "I have no idea what you're talking about. Why would I tell you or not tell you about Daphne?"

"Because!" Katherine said, and her voice broke. She felt tears in her eyes. She had promised herself she wasn't going to do things like that in front of Colin anymore. "Fuck," she said, and wiped them away.

"Katherine," Colin said, "I see what you're driving at, of course, and I can promise you that I haven't the least interest in Daphne or anyone else for that matter. You know that."

Katherine said, "You seem to know a lot about her."

"What? That she's a studio art major? That she transferred from Towson State? That her mother is chair of the art history department at Bucknell?"

"See!"

Colin laughed. "I'm only pointing out how I know a little something about everyone in workshop, as we tend to be a tight-knit bunch without quite stepping over into a full-blown orgy. At least, not yet anyway."

"Now you're trying to be absurd."

"Oh, I'm not," Colin said. "I'm only wishing to let you know that I am friends with several members of the female sex common to a young man in his first year in college. But I thought those relationships seemed tangential to ours, although I'm beginning to see that I was wrong, and wish now to make a full and proper disclosure."

"You're just trying to cover up," Katherine said. "About Daphne."

"I am in occasional conversation with one Ashley," Colin said, "who serves the English Club in her capacity as secretary, and whose minutes are, from time to time, tardy, requiring me to telephone her at her place of residence and speed her along."

"See?" Katherine said. "You're just trying to steer the conversation away from Daphne."

"I would also like to disclose," Colin continued, "that, last Tuesday, I believe, I was accosted by one Susan, who was in need of the notes from our last sociology class, and offered to pay me cash money to photocopy mine."

Katherine put her face in the pillow and cried. "You know what you're doing," she said. "You know."

Colin began to stroke her hair. "Come on, Katherine," he said. "Let's not do this, OK? It's so . . . mainstream."

"Why did she paint that stupid bike lock?"

"Let's not do this," Colin said. "I don't want to do this; you don't want to do this, OK?" He began kissing her.

"And why did you tell everyone your story was true?" Katherine said. "What were you thinking?"

Colin stopped kissing her. "Because it is true," he said, "in a way."

"In what way? The untrue way?"

"No," Colin said. He told her it was difficult to explain. The truth, in fiction, was a rich tapestry whose elegant and elaborate folds were often impossible to smooth out. "The best I can do is say that it is emotionally true if not quite literally true."

"Well, your class took it as being literally true."

Colin shrugged. "I leave that for the reader."

"And why didn't your professor introduce me to the class?"

"Why would he?"

"Because I was sitting there in class with you for over an hour while you guys fought about symbols and allegories and vivid dreams."

"I believe you are referring to Gardner's 'vivid and continuous dream,'" Colin said. "But forgive me, and forgive my professor if we didn't realize that enduring such discussions warranted one a class introduction."

"I didn't say I *endured* anything. I just felt stupid sitting there without anyone saying anything to me. That's all."

"But that doesn't seem to be all," Colin said. "No, you act like you're entitled to something."

"Stop turning this around on me! Did you even tell your professor that I was coming to class?"

Colin began kissing her along her neck. "I seem to recall mentioning something to him about it at some point."

"Meaning you did or did not tell him I would be coming to class today?"

"Meaning," Colin said, "he seemed agreeable to whatever I proposed initially. And, since I had ascertained his initial agreeableness, any further discussion on the matter would have been superfluous, wouldn't it?"

Katherine wanted to punch things. She wanted to punch big and heavy things until they collapsed in their bigness and heaviness and came up gasping for air. She would punch their gasping, too. She wanted to rip Daphne's copy of Colin's story in half, which Daphne had decorated with elaborate drawings of scenes from the story. Katherine wanted to punch Daphne. She wanted to punch Daphne as Colin looked on. With Daphne's shredded manuscript clutched sorrowfully in his tear-soaked hands. And then she wanted to punch Colin, because why not?

But she didn't punch Colin. She didn't rip Daphne's manuscript. Instead, Katherine and Colin ended up doing it. Even though Colin was still talking about his workshop, complaining how the class couldn't understand the simplest things, the most obvious parallels. It was like they hadn't even *read* the story, you know? Even though Colin finished too quickly and apologized. Even though Katherine ended up crying because Colin always had to turn everything into something about him—everything—like she wasn't even there, really, except to be the dutiful recipient of his apologies and console him time and time again. Even though Colin launched into a five-minute soliloquy whose chief theme seemed to be I Turn Everything into Something About Me Because You Make Me Turn Everything into Something About Me. Even though it was getting late and Katherine would be late getting home, they did it anyway, the way they would always end up doing it from now to the end of their relationship, closer than Katherine would think. Colin would break up with her a few months later. Katherine would see it coming except for how she totally didn't. Colin would say he didn't know what it was. He just wanted to be alone, that's all. Too much schoolwork. Too much pressure. Too much everything. She'd understand, he promised her, when she got to college.

And Katherine did. For, a year later, Katherine entered college and slept with three men for whom she had little feeling, although she would end up in the hospital after the third one dumped her, the least significant of the three, really, a boy so unworthy of Katherine's affections as to summon them in abundance, Katherine following the boy to class and to his apartment, which looked out over the deli where he worked and where Katherine sometimes stopped after class, even after getting out of the hospital, even after the boy threatened to call the police on Katherine, who only wished to explain her true feelings for him, which, if not literally true, were emotionally so, and wasn't that really the same thing? It was, the boy's hand across her face told her. It was.

LUCKY US

On the day Miriam bit a man for trying to steal her fried chicken, she and her granddaughter, Leaf, watched Minibike Boy jump the ramp. Leaf lived with Miriam, as did Miriam's daughter, Sadie, who had recently moved back into Miriam's house while she separated from her husband. Sadie promised to find her own place soon, but Miriam had her doubts, gray, shapeless visitors that seemed to hover between them and cloud Miriam's eyesight. Twice since Sadie had moved back in Miriam thought she saw a blue dot scurry across the kitchen floor, only to see it later ascending the bathroom wall. It was nothing, of course. One of those things you saw from time to time and knew not to worry about. Still, Miriam let out a cry when she saw the dot scale Sadie's neck in the middle of one of their meals together.

"What is it?" Sadie asked.

"Nothing," Miriam said.

"Is there something on me?" Sadie put down her fork and brushed her shoulders. "I've been seeing a lot of ladybugs in here lately."

"It's not a ladybug," Miriam said.

"Do you know when the last time you said that to me was? When I was eight years old. I woke up in the middle of the night and found one crawling on my pillow. I ran screaming into your room.

Remember? And you said, 'Go back to sleep, it's not a ladybug,' and I said yes it was, there's no mistaking a ladybug. And you said, 'Well, they don't hurt anything. Go back to sleep.' I wanted you to come into my room and see it, but you wouldn't."

Miriam needed a moment for this one. She sipped her ice water and considered this ladybug of Sadie's youth, still clinging to its symbolic import, whatever that was for Sadie. Anything she wanted it to be, she thought. Miriam said, "Sorry."

"You don't have to be *sorry,*" Sadie said. "I wasn't asking for an apology."

"I should have come to see the ladybug."

"That's not what I was saying."

"Sorry."

"I don't want an apology!"

"I'm sorry for apologizing, then."

"Jesus," Sadie said. "What do you think I am? Some little kid who still wants to make her mommy feel bad about her gloomy childhood?"

Well, now that you mention it, Miriam thought. "Was it really? Gloomy, I mean."

Sadie closed her eyes and let out an exasperated sigh. "I'm not falling for it, Mom. I'm not. You want to fight; it's obvious. Well, I won't let it happen."

"I don't want to fight," Miriam said.

"She said," Sadie said, "loading her gun."

"I was only asking a question."

"She said, taking aim."

"I wasn't taking aim at anything."

"She said—

"Stop saying 'she said'!" Miriam said. They ate in silence.

After a while Sadie said, "Well, you got what you wanted."

* * *

Minibike Boy lived a few blocks from Miriam, in a ranch house typically rented out to college kids, changing beery hands every fall, or so it seemed to Miriam on those occasions when she drove by, a FOR RENT sign crookedly impaled upon the weedy lawn. There were hundreds of houses like these in town, Miriam knew, but her neighborhood had been spared for the most part, still enough seniors and empty nesters to keep the local college at bay. Minibike Boy wasn't in college, though. Miriam had seen Minibike Boy's mother loading groceries from their ancient minivan; another time she'd seen Minibike Boy's sister bouncing impossibly high on the trampoline that materialized where the FOR RENT sign used to be. The girl was smoking a cigarette.

On the day Minibike Boy jumped the ramp, Leaf stayed home from school. Said she really wasn't sick, didn't want to lie about it, but didn't want to go to school either, where she was certain to fail a math test without an extra day to study. Could she stay home just this one time? Please? Miriam, who had already decided she'd let Leaf stay after she admitted she wasn't sick, gave Leaf a lecture about responsibility and told her she could study at the kitchen table. Let her study in her room and you might as well drop her off at the mall. Let Leaf be in the middle of things, where she sometimes thrived. Keep an eye out, but keep your distance, too. Leaf was fifteen years old.

Outside, Minibike Boy assembled a ramp in the middle of the road. An old door propped against two cinder blocks. Miriam watched him from the kitchen window, this kid dragging a heavy door down the street. He wore a purple motorcycle helmet and flip-flops. Leaf sat at the table and drank the peppermint tea Miriam had recently gotten her into. She had a textbook, a notebook, and a sketch pad spread out before her. Sometimes it freed her up a little, drawing something while she studied.

"What's that noise?" Leaf asked.

Miriam told her.

"Oh."

"Looks like he's got some kind of ramp today."

"Really?" Leaf stood from the table. "Where?"

"Don't pay it any mind," Miriam said, but Leaf had already walked to the window.

"Wow, that's a bad idea," she said admiringly.

"Worst part is we'll be the ones to call the ambulance," Miriam said.

Together they watched Minibike Boy. He revved his motor at the end of the street and approached the ramp without going over it. Instead, he slowed to a stop, his uncertain feet touching the door, waiting, testing things out. He repeated this several times. The minibike made a noise like a chainsaw. The boy circled the ramp, sped down the street, and returned again. His helmet glinted in the sun.

"He's scared," Leaf said.

"Should be," Miriam said.

A moment later Minibike Boy circled the block—they could hear him traveling behind their house and around the corner, the neighborhood dead at this time of morning.

"I bet we're the only ones watching," Miriam said.

"He doesn't even know."

"Lucky us."

He sped past the ramp again. Stopped at the end of the street and revved the bike a few more times. Waiting.

"Working up his stupidity," Miriam said.

Leaf said, "I feel bad for him."

"I'll say something," Miriam volunteered.

"Be nice, though," Leaf said.

"What do you mean 'though'?" Miriam said.

Outside, Miriam walked to the edge of her lawn, a retiree out to check her mail before it arrived. Minibike Boy didn't seem embarrassed by her presence, as Miriam hoped he might when she first crossed the lawn and saw him glance at her beneath his helmeted head. Poor kid. She opened her empty mailbox, peered inside. "Hello," she said, and waved to Minibike Boy, but Minibike Boy couldn't hear her, she realized. He revved his engine and slowly circled the ramp.

"Looks like you've built yourself a ramp," Miriam shouted.

Minibike Boy looked at her blankly.

"I said it looks like you've built yourself a ramp."

Minibike Boy nodded.

"My name is Miriam. I live here." With my granddaughter, she nearly said, then decided against it. "We saw you."

Minibike Boy didn't say anything.

"Do you live a few blocks over?"

Minibike Boy revved his engine.

"I think I've seen you over there sometimes. Riding around."

Minibike Boy looked at her.

"Do you think you might keep it down? Just a little? Or maybe not ride so close to people's homes? Maybe there's a track or something like that, someplace nearby?"

Minibike Boy struck the pose of a scolded child, head down, shoulders slumped.

"It's a little noisy," Miriam said, but Minibike Boy suddenly pulled away. Disappeared around the corner. Miriam turned to the window where Leaf was regarding her with clear disapproval, but how could she know what had been said? It wasn't like she'd embarrassed him by saying why don't you quit before you kill yourself, which was the first thing that came to mind. She'd been nice.

"I was nice," she said.

Leaf stared back at her and pointed.

"What?" Miriam said, but then she understood. Minibike Boy had rounded the block, returning, engine revving high. Miriam could feel it in her chest. A few moments later she saw him, fingers gripping the minibike's slender handlebars, his body crouched low. Heading straight for the ramp.

"Don't," Miriam said.

But he did. He rode past her and ascended the ramp in an instant—zip!—landing safely on the other side. The ramp shook in his wake. The bike bounced and juddered. Minibike Boy rode on, his purple helmet catching the sun, the air charged with a fragrance of gasoline, exhaust, and rubber. Miriam watched him ride away. For the moment he'd been suspended in midair—the minibike's back wheel free, the front not yet landed—Miriam had felt a pleasant terror, as on a vacation morning early in her marriage when she and her husband had eaten breakfast on a foreign balcony and Ron had said what's that behind you at the very moment she turned to greet the hummingbird fluttering an inch from her face, its furious wings beating her nose the instant before her breath returned.

"He did it," Miriam said. She turned to the kitchen window. "He did it!"

Leaf's expression conveyed neither pleasure nor disappointment.

"He jumped it!"

Leaf moved away from the window, returning Miriam to her lawn, the street, and the ordinariness of her heart beating through her chest.

That evening Miriam bought a fried chicken dinner and went to the Laundromat to wash an oversized comforter Sadie had unwisely jammed inside their washing machine. Miriam hadn't had fried food since Sadie moved in, injecting the house with organic produce and hypoallergenic shampoo. She would get to eat this chicken in private, she realized, without Sadie there to say, "Do you know what's *in* that?" the way she did when Miriam and Leaf ate ice cream sandwiches while watching *Jeopardy!* Sadie had instructed her to buy unscented detergent. Isn't all detergent unscented? Miriam had asked, to which Sadie had said of course not, Mom, what do you think Tide smells like, and Miriam had said, "Tide. Tide smells like Tide," and Sadie had said right, so it must be *scented,* and Miriam decided not to say anything, although she would have liked to say that she was glad Tide smelled like Tide, scented or not, since that was often the only way to tell if clothes were clean. Who wanted unscented cleanliness?

She needed quarters. The machine was at the back of the Laundromat, near the bathrooms Miriam couldn't imagine anyone using. A mother and her baby were getting quarters, the mother smoothing a wrinkled dollar into compliance. As she approached, Miriam gave the baby a smile, but the baby regarded her blankly, seated in a shopping cart that had wandered in from wherever. A few moments later the machine swallowed her dollars and noisily spit out change. "Jackpot," Miriam said, not loud enough for anyone to hear. The quarters, heavy in the machine's hooded dish, summoned an image of the Sunday collection plate, which always seemed to hold an embarrassment of coins. Who were these people who came to Mass loaded down with change, like retirees to Atlantic City?

Miriam ate her chicken and waited. The Laundromat had gotten nearly empty, aside from a woman in sweatpants who seemed to make a game of switching a load, leaving the Laundromat, returning, switching a load, leaving, all while talking on her cell phone. "You act," Miriam heard her say, in passing, "like you've never had anyone throw pretzels at you before." It hadn't occurred to Miriam to be afraid, alone in a Laundromat, but now the idea seemed worth considering. There was a drop-off window that looked like it hadn't been used in years. Half the top-loading washers had OUT OF ORDER signs duct-taped across their fronts; the first three dryers Miriam tried were missing their lint screens.

She was just about to eat the last piece of chicken when the two boys came in. That's how Miriam would forever describe them, *the two boys,* although they were probably older than she first realized: so many adults wore their clothes baggy, with oversized hoodies disguising their faces, as one of these did. Both were over six feet, with chains sagging from their belt loops to their back pockets, which hung level with their hips, their boxers showing. They came in through the front doors and walked to the change machine. One wore a blue hoodie, beneath which Miriam could see a goatee and a pair of lips whose bottom half was impaled by a silver stud. The other wore a gray sweatshirt, his hair in a chunky braid so blond it was white. On his way to the change machine, Sweatshirt kicked a dryer door closed, an idea Hoodie quickly imitated, loudly kicking other doors. "Wait," Sweatshirt said. He crouched down and pulled a beach towel out of an open dryer. "Oh shit," he said, "check this out." He opened the towel to reveal an image of Tony the Tiger flying an airplane while holding an enormous bowl of Frosted Flakes.

"Who the fuck's that?" Hoodie said.

"You serious?" Sweatshirt said. "*They're grrrreat!*"

"Thing's gross. Some kid probably puked on it."

"It's Tony the Tiger," Sweatshirt said.

"Tony the who?"

"Tony the Tiger. Frosted Flakes. You don't know Tony the Tiger?"

"We were strict Apple Jacks," Hoodie said. "A is for apple."

"Oh, yeah, Apple Jacks," Sweatshirt said.

"You'd drink the milk," Hoodie said. "After."

"Those little pink things," Sweatshirt said.

"Floating around," Hoodie agreed.

Miriam watched them shove a dollar into the machine and wondered whether they were high.

"You got to do it all in one motion," Sweatshirt said.

"I am."

"You're not. Like this, see?"

Miriam could see that they'd taped the dollar at one end, doubling its length, making it possible to insert it into the machine and retract it, again and again.

"That's how I was doing it," Hoodie said.

"You were doing it stupid," Sweatshirt said, and then Hoodie said something Miriam couldn't hear. A few moments later Hoodie walked out the front door, angry. Sweatshirt fed the dollar into the machine and collected the change in a plastic grocery bag. Miriam wasn't sure if she should call someone; she had her cell phone in her purse, but almost never used it. She was trying to decide what to do when Sweatshirt turned around and spotted her. He put the dollar away and shoved the last fistful of change into the bag. When he came and stood before her, Miriam grasped that he'd been drinking.

"That your dinner?" he asked.

Miriam nodded.

"Don't lie," Sweatshirt said. He offered his notion of a playful grin. His eyes were like punched holes.

Miriam felt fear wash over her. "Oh, I wouldn't—"

"Don't say it is if it isn't," Sweatshirt said.

"No, of course I—"

"Don't say a yes that's a no."

"No, I mean, yes. Right." She could see his yellow teeth.

"'Cause we know it's not a yes," Sweatshirt said. "We know it's a no."

"Well—"

"'Cause we know it's mine."

You can have it if you want, Miriam was about to say, when Sweatshirt swung the bag of coins and struck her on the leg. Miriam cried out, more in fear than pain. How strange her cry sounded— she had no idea she still could, really.

Sweatshirt grabbed her chicken dinner.

"No!" Miriam clutched the box to her chest as if it were her purse.

"Give it," Sweatshirt said. The box began to tear.

"No!"

Where was everyone in this town that no one could be inside the Laundromat when a sixty-three-year-old woman was being attacked for a chicken breast and a half-eaten dinner roll? "You can't have it!" she must have yelled, for that's what the cell phone woman later told her she said, after Sweatshirt had run through the front doors, clutching the garbage bag and holding his arm to his mouth. After the woman asked her if she needed to use her cell phone. After she'd asked Miriam what had happened.

And this is what had happened: Miriam bit him. With her *teeth*! With her incisors, still slick with chicken grease. She bit him when he leaned his weight into her. The moment after he scooped his arms around the chicken box, like a linebacker stripping the ball from a rookie back. "You can't have it!" The sweatshirt's sleeves were baggy and loose, pulling away from his arm, exposing a weakness. But she hadn't thought of it as a weakness. She hadn't thought anything at all, really, save this: she couldn't disappoint this maniac woman who was shouting, "You can't have it!" She couldn't. So she bit him. He dropped the box and screamed. The cell phone woman materialized from wherever, still holding her phone. "Hey!" she said. "Hey!" She held the phone out, about to click a photograph of him, but Sweatshirt turned away, looking at the crazy woman clutching a fried chicken box to her chest. For a moment, his eyes met hers, and he understood: he wouldn't get her dinner after all. He couldn't have it.

Well, she had told him.

"You bit him?" Sadie asked.

"Just barely," Miriam said.

"You bit a human being," Sadie said, flatly.

"He was," Miriam agreed. "Just barely."

They were sitting in the living room, the laundry bags on a coffee table before them, Sadie removing her clothes from the rest. Leaf's clothes would be left for Miriam to fold and put away, as always. Since Sadie had moved in, these occurrences had cropped up more and more, even when Leaf was in the room, as she was now, drawing something in front of the television.

"Well," Sadie said. "Human enough to have some disease."

"I don't think so," Miriam said.

Sadie shrugged. "You'd be surprised," she said.

"Yes," Miriam agreed. "Whoever he is, he should be worried."

Sadie gave her a look. "Do you know," she said, "that it is nearly impossible to have a conversation with you? I mean a serious, adult conversation, like the kind I could have with anyone my age. I think I should be able to have one with my own mother, but when she reduces my concerns to a joke, I discover I'm wrong."

"Why should who be worried?" Leaf asked. "About what?"

"The man in the Laundromat," Miriam said. "Your mother thinks I might have given him a terrible disease."

"Did you?"

"Not that I'm aware of."

"Oh," Leaf said, turning back to the television.

"Your grandmother is only teasing," Sadie said. "She wants you to think she's amusing."

"Aren't I?" Miriam countered, but Sadie didn't say anything. On the television, groups of teens raced around the world, some reality show Miriam had yet to warm up to. Sometimes Leaf could turn her on to something really good—Miriam was surprised to discover that Leaf enjoyed a good PBS miniseries as much as she did—but other times it was a losing proposition. The teenagers in tonight's show were always yelling at one another. That seemed the point of the entire show, teens yelling in front of a world monument, then on to the next monument, more yelling.

Leaf had one of her drawing pads out, using the charcoals she really wasn't supposed to use in the living room, but oh well. Lately she'd been doing some good work with the charcoals. She'd done a still life of Miriam's fruit bowl that Miriam thought might fetch a few dollars at her church's Fall Festival, but Leaf wasn't interested. Miriam didn't argue and instead had hung the drawing on the refrigerator.

"Give me a break," Sadie said, responding to something happening on the TV show. "What a bunch of idiots." She stood from the table and carried a pile of clothes to her room; Miriam watched her go, then stole a glance at Leaf's drawing and saw she was drawing a person. Miriam knew better than to ask Leaf about it—Leaf was painfully shy—but wait her out a bit and she might show you. At my own speed, Leaf's actions seemed to say. I'll come to you, eventually.

After a while, Miriam said, "What are you working on there?"

Leaf showed Miriam the drawing. "It's him," she explained, "the guy who bit you."

Miriam looked at the drawing, a man in dark sunglasses and a sweatshirt. A thin mustache. Two scars. "Wow, he's really scary," Miriam said. "But honey, he didn't bite me; I bit him."

"Oh."

"But he probably would have bitten me if he had the chance."

"Oh." Leaf gave Miriam a disappointed look. "I thought you said he bit you."

"Nope," Miriam said, "but it sure did feel that way." And it did. That's how she felt, bitten by this strange boy with his bagful of stolen coins. Like he'd taken a little part of her. Had Leaf intuited that somehow? Had she glimpsed Miriam's secret heart? For there was a part of the story Miriam would never include, in all the retellings. It happened after Sweatshirt had screamed out in pain, clutching his arm to his chest. The moment before he darted out the front doors, he'd looked at Miriam as if she were someone who contained surprising depths. Someone worthy, even, of his worthless respect.

He'd winked at her. Sweatshirt had winked at her.

When Sadie was in kindergarten, Miriam would sometimes spy on her at recess. The kindergarten, a Depression-era schoolhouse with tall, double-hung windows looking out across a playground fitted out with a jungle gym, sliding board, swings, and a four-square court, was close enough to Miriam's home that nearly every errand occasioned driving by, often in the midafternoon, when Sadie's class was outside, playing. Miriam would drive around the playground once, trying to eye Sadie, and then circle around again, because she wanted to and because who would ever know? She'd slow the car into a parking space across from the playground and cut the engine. She'd roll the windows down. She'd hear shouts, laughter, the creak and sigh of swings. The pinging echo of a basketball inexpertly dribbled.

And then she would see Sadie. Sadie would walk along the fence that bordered the playground. She'd drag a stick along the fence's rusty links, making a noise Miriam, in her station wagon with the windows down, could just barely hear. Sometimes a friend would accompany Sadie—more often, not. Miriam was able to see Sadie's face, but not to read the expression there, which was neither cheerful nor sad. Sometimes it seemed that Sadie was singing; sometimes Sadie's lips were drawn tight. Miriam watched, wondering what to think about Sadie's recess routine: should she be worried that Sadie did not seem to play with the other children? Should she talk to Sadie's teacher? But no, that would only embarrass Sadie and fuel her anger toward her mother, an anger that already seemed out of proportion for a five-year-old. An anger that was already shaping itself into the puzzle that would stump Miriam for years to come.

So she tried talking to Sadie. She'd ask Sadie how school was today. Fine, Sadie would say. Well, what did she do today? Anything fun? Sadie would shrug and say she couldn't remember. Nothing? Really? Sadie wouldn't say anything. How about recess? Miriam would say. What did you play at recess?

Sadie turned a face on Miriam that Miriam could not read. "Swings," Sadie said. "I played on the swings." Or, "I played kickball." Or, "I chased bugs with Anna." Or, "We didn't have recess today because it was too cold outside."

One day Miriam parked her car in the parking space and rolled her window all the way down. It was October, but still warm enough to go outside without a jacket. She could see Sadie dragging her stick along the fence, could see Sadie's blank expression, as cheerless as the sound of the stick against the links. When Sadie drew closer, Miriam did something that surprised herself: she called out to Sadie. "Sadie," she said. "Hi, Sadie. Over here. It's me, Mommy."

Sadie looked around until her eyes met Miriam's. Her mouth was a quickly sketched line.

"Hi," Miriam said. "Surprise."

Sadie didn't say anything.

"That's a pretty neat stick you've got, isn't it?"

Sadie looked away.

"Maybe you can bring it home tonight and show me?"

Sadie continued dragging her stick along the fence. She dragged it until a teacher called the children inside and Sadie dropped her stick in the grass and ran as fast as Miriam had ever seen her run, across the playground and up the stairs, where a teacher waited at the top, a teacher who ruffled Sadie's hair the moment she passed inside and then closed the door behind the last child and returned Miriam's attention to the car waiting to take her parking spot.

After she'd finished folding the laundry, Miriam sat with Leaf in front of the television, not really watching, but not wanting to turn the TV off, either. It began to get dark outside; Miriam could just see the lone streetlight at the end of her block, visible through the window above the television.

And then she heard it: Minibike Boy's minibike outside. Leaf gave her a look. "What is he doing out now?" she said. Miriam stood from the sofa and went to the kitchen window.

"He's out there," she said. "Riding around."

"Let me see," Leaf said. She joined Miriam at the window. They could both see Minibike Boy passing by at top speed, his minibike wanly illuminated by a weak headlight.

"It's a flashlight," Miriam said.

"He's going to kill himself," Leaf said.

"Who's going to kill himself?" Sadie said, materializing behind them. She held a stack of folded towels to her chest, which she placed on the kitchen table before joining them at the window.

"Minibike Boy," Leaf said.

"Minibike Boy?" Sadie said. She leaned closer to the window and cupped her hand to the glass. "Who is Minibike Boy?"

"He's some kid who rides around the neighborhood on a mini-bike," Leaf explained, but no explanation was necessary, as Minibike Boy zoomed by, the flashlight atop his handlebars bobbing up and down. Across the street, house lights began to flicker on.

"Jesus," Sadie said. "Why don't you stop him?"

"We tried," Miriam said.

"This morning," Leaf confirmed.

"There was a ramp," Miriam said.

Sadie looked at them. It was the same look Sadie once gave Miriam when Miriam told her she wouldn't let Leaf wear the tie-dyed halter top Sadie had made for her at an art colony, the one week Sadie had moved away with a painter she'd met online, an event, Miriam gently argued, she probably wouldn't want Leaf to memorialize. "What is wrong with you people?" Sadie said.

"Lots, probably," Miriam said.

"What do you two do all day?" Sadie said. A moment later she opened the front door and crossed the front lawn in her bare feet, waving her arms whenever Minibike Boy zipped past. Miriam and Leaf joined her, Miriam noting a few neighbors watching them from their front porches. Minibike Boy gave Sadie a look the next time he passed by, swerving out of her way as she stood in the street with her arms out, as if to say stop, halt. "Are you crazy?" she shouted as he passed by, but Minibike Boy only sped away.

"He can't hear you," Miriam said.

"Too loud," Leaf said, but Sadie didn't say anything. The next time Minibike Boy passed, though, he'd slowed down enough that Sadie could do something that surprised them all: she grabbed the minibike's handlebars and began running alongside it, shouting,

"Stop! Now!" More surprising: Minibike Boy complied. He idled the bike to a stop as Sadie held the minibike like a defeated bull. When Minibike Boy turned the engine off and stood from the bike, Sadie grabbed him by one arm and dragged him across the front yard. "What's your problem?" she yelled, but Minibike Boy only kicked his legs and hung his helmeted head. "What were you thinking?" Sadie led him to the front porch; Minibike Boy didn't resist.

"God, don't embarrass him, Mom," Leaf said.

"Too late for that," Sadie said.

"She's right," Miriam said, and Sadie looked at her with surprise. "Your mom did the right thing." She looked at Sadie and said, "The neighbors are watching, though; let's get him inside before you read him the riot act."

Sadie said, "OK."

Inside, they sat Minibike Boy down at the kitchen table. He'd cut his leg somehow—perhaps, Miriam feared, when Sadie had pulled him from the bike—and Miriam handed him a damp washcloth to wipe away the blood. She could see his eyes through the helmet's shield, but it wasn't until he removed the helmet and placed it on his lap that they saw his face, older than she'd imagined, pale as an underarm and crowned with an unfashionable bowl cut, badly in need of a trim, hanging unevenly in his eyes. "Thanks for that, miss," he said, indicating the towel.

"Are you British or something?" Leaf asked.

"Born there," he said. "Moved here when I was nine."

"What were you doing riding around on that stupid bike?" Sadie said. "At night!"

Minibike Boy fumbled nervously with his helmet. "Very sorry about that," he said.

"You could have gotten yourself killed!"

Minibike Boy flipped the helmet's shield up and down in a desultory way. "Yes, I know," he said. "Not something I'm proud of, really."

"Where are your parents?" Miriam asked.

"Give me their number," Sadie said.

"What's your name?" Leaf asked.

Minibike Boy smiled a crooked smile and said, "Last one's easiest, isn't it? My name's Basil."

"Family name?" Miriam offered.

"How else do you get named Basil?" Basil said.

"We call you Minibike Boy," Leaf volunteered.

"Minibike Boy?" Basil said. "Bit impersonal, isn't it?"

"Listen," Sadie said. She pointed a finger at Basil's chest. "If I ever catch you riding that fucking minibike through the neighborhood at night again, I'm going to call the police. Got it?"

"Mom!" Leaf said. "You don't have to be so mean to him!"

"No," Basil said, "your mom is right. I deserve it." He folded up the washcloth and handed it to Miriam. "Not sure if you want this back, really," he said.

"That's fine," Miriam said. "I'll take it."

"I'm sorry I disturbed you all this evening," Basil said. "I didn't mean to. I really didn't. Usually I keep to myself. I'm actually quite shy. My aunt says she doesn't know what to do with me, but mostly I don't give her any trouble. That's who I live with, my aunt. Plus my cousin, Annabelle. She's a nice kid, but she likes to test my aunt, every once in a while. You know, see what her limits are. It gets tough being around all that after a while, but it's not too bad. Not terrible. I mean, it was kind of my aunt to take me in and I know it must be difficult for Annabelle to have me around, but I try to be a big brother to her, in a way. I like that. Makes me feel good when I can look out for her. Makes me happy, you know? But sometimes I start to feel sad about things for no real reason and the more I start to feel sad the sadder and sadder I get until it's just like there's nothing I can do to stop the sad feeling and riding around on that silly bike seems to help somehow." He rested his hands atop the helmet. "I don't know how to explain it."

"I think I get it," Leaf said.

"You do?"

"Yeah," Leaf said.

"Thanks," Basil said.

For a moment Miriam was afraid Sadie was going to light into him again, but Sadie only stood from the table and said, "Well, we'd better get you home."

Basil nodded. "Thanks, everyone," he said. "And apologies, too."

The three of them walked him to the door, where Sadie told them she'd walk him home to make sure he got home safely.

"Oh, I'd hate to be a bother," Basil said.

"Too late," Sadie said, but there was no anger in it. Miriam watched as Basil picked up his minibike and walked it with Sadie, Sadie holding one handlebar, from which Basil had hung his purple helmet. She and Leaf watched them in the streetlight, Sadie laughing at something Basil was saying, the night drawing in around them. Later, when Sadie returned from her errand, Miriam remembered to ask her what Basil said that made her laugh, and Sadie said, "He said we seemed like a happy family."

THINK OF ME AND I'LL KNOW

A few days after I lost my job, my son's cat disappeared. We'd gotten him the cat when he was five, my wife's idea. That was a few years ago when we'd first moved out here so I could take a job at the paper mill. Don't ask me about the paper mill. If there's anything I don't want to talk about it's the paper mill. My wife thought a pet might be a good idea for Joshua. Said she thought he felt lonely; maybe a cat would do the trick. She'd always had cats around, growing up. She said she missed having them curl up at her ankles while she drifted off to sleep. Me, I'm more of a dog person. Give me a good dog any day over a cat, I said.

But my wife didn't listen.

We looked everywhere for the right cat. *Everywhere.* Pet shelters, pet stores, classifieds, neighbors, coworkers eager to unload another unwanted kitty. But each time my wife found something wrong with them: this one was too aggressive, that one too frail, the other one would never learn to trust a child. My wife saw imperfections where I wouldn't even think to look. She'd tell Joshua she was sorry, but we'd know when we found the right one. She was sure of it. Joshua didn't say anything. Who knows what he thought? It's still hard to tell what Joshua is thinking a lot of the time.

After a while, we stopped talking about getting a cat altogether, which was just fine with me. I settled into my terrible job, my wife found work proofing classifieds, and Joshua trudged off to kindergarten, his book bag heavy with a thermos and lunch box. My wife used to write little notes on his napkin, which I always said was cute, but really they embarrassed me. I didn't like the idea of teachers watching Joshua wipe his face with a napkin that said *We're so super-duper proud of YOU!* in my wife's exuberant script. What would they think about her, about us? Sometimes, when it was my turn to drive Joshua to school, I'd slip the napkin out of his lunchbox. "Whoa there, buddy," I'd say, pretending to rearrange his cream cheese sandwich and apple wedges. Then I'd stuff the napkin into my pocket. I'd drop Joshua off at the kindergarten door, where he'd let me kiss him without quite kissing me back. Joshua has never really been much into kissing.

It was me who found the cat originally. I was hanging out with a couple of my buddies, drinking beer on a Saturday when I was supposed to be taking the recycling to the dump, when—and this is the part I still can't believe—a cat walked right up to me and put its paws against my legs. We were sitting outside in fold-up chairs, talking about everything and nothing, when I heard one of my buddies say, "Looks like you got yourself a friend." On the drive home, the cat put his paws to the passenger window. When my wife asked me where I found the cat, I said, "He found *me.*"

Joshua named him Chessie. Not the name I would have picked, but Chessie liked it right away. He'd follow Joshua around from room to room, come when Joshua called him down to dinner. At night Chessie would sleep at my wife's ankles, just the way she wanted, but I always hated the feeling of it. Like someone was sitting at the foot of your bed, watching. One night when I was having trouble sleeping—I'm always having trouble sleeping—I picked up Chessie and carried him into the hallway. "Go," I said, and dumped him outside the bedroom door. When I got back to bed, though, Chessie was already there, curled at my wife's ankles. Asleep.

My wife was married once before, but it only lasted a week. As in seven days. That's it. It's not something my wife will talk about anymore, but she used to tell me things, back when we were first dating, the kinds of things you discuss when you're first dating. I didn't mind about her being married before, especially since I almost got married right out of high school, but didn't. God, I'm glad I didn't get married right out of high school. Of all the things I'm glad about, not getting married right out of high school is the thing I'm most glad about.

Anyway, Ian was the guy's name, the guy my wife was married to for one week. I've never liked anyone named Ian, but I didn't tell my wife that. They met at work, back when my wife worked for the phone company. My wife was a phone operator. Remember those? Nobody talks to the operator anymore. But my wife was a good operator, kept getting these little promotions in the company, until she was in charge of a team of operators. And Ian was one of them, I guess, that's how they met. I can see them meeting, the way you always seem to meet people at work. People you end up sleeping with, or dating, or, in my wife's case, marrying for one week. I can see them hanging out, going out to lunch maybe, offering each other a ride home—things like that. I can see Ian making fun of everything, the thing my wife used to like about me back when we were first together. He was probably like me, I imagine. I've always been kind of good at making fun of everything, but I guess that's not something to brag about once you hit a certain age. Once you hit a certain age you just sound bitter, making fun of everything. At least that's what my wife has said to me more times than I'd like to hear. She's got a point; I'll give her that. But which would you rather have, a point or a husband who can still make fun of everything?

They honeymooned in Virginia Beach. Not my favorite place in the world, but they were young and didn't have much money, so I can't blame them (my wife and I didn't really have a honeymoon, to be honest, unless you count the time her parents invited us to their time-share in Santa Fe. "It's your honeymoon!" they said. But they were there, with us, sipping margaritas, so call it what you want, I say). They stayed in a nice enough hotel, went out to restaurants and bars, and tried spending an afternoon on the beach, although Ian burned easily and had to avoid the sun, so why Virginia Beach, I thought, but didn't say anything. You could just as easily go to the Poconos. Hot in the summer, but plenty of shade. Mini golf.

Right away my wife knew something was wrong, but she didn't know what it was. "He was acting strange," she told me. "Like, we'd go out for a big starchy breakfast, you know, after a morning of sex, but Ian would just order a bagel and a coffee, but he wouldn't even finish the bagel. He'd just take a few bites and make these pretend smiles at me, but when I'd ask him if anything was wrong, he'd say of course not, or he was just tired, or this coffee hasn't kicked in yet. But what he'd do most of the time was not say anything at all. He'd just drink his coffee and look out the window like he was expecting someone to come meet him and take him away. He'd excuse himself to go to the bathroom and come back thirty minutes later with no explanation whatsoever"—I was really tempted to make a joke about that, but didn't—"and I'd say, 'Is everything OK?' and he'd say it was. Then I'd say, 'Because it seems like something's on your mind,' and he'd say there wasn't. He'd pick at his bagel without eating it, and then we'd go outside into the sun, where he'd put on this enormous sun hat and sunglasses and stare out at the ocean, which was full of jellyfish, that week we were there. It was in all the papers; they put signs up on the beach. I don't think we ever waded in past our ankles."

"Maybe he left because of the jellyfish," I said.

My wife gave me a look when I said that.

"You never know," I said.

But my wife said, "The funny thing was, the day he left I already knew it was coming because he'd taken a pen out of my purse and put it back in the wrong place, and I knew what he was up to. Like that." My wife snapped her fingers. "It was like I saw the pen in the wrong place and thought, 'Ian took the pen to write me a Dear John letter which I'll find tomorrow after he leaves,' in the blink of an eye."

"In the blink of an eye," I said. "I've always liked that expression." But as soon as I said it, I knew it was a mistake, because my wife stopped telling me about Ian. She looked out the window where trees were starting to bend in the wind.

"Rain," she said.

A few days after Chessie disappeared, I went out pretending to look for jobs. That's something I do sometimes. Makes me feel like I'm still *in it* somehow, like things are about to improve. I ended up at the library with the idea of searching online, but spent most of my time browsing the dollar cart instead. The library keeps the dollar cart outside, even when it rains, mostly old computer manuals, tax guides, and romances that even people who read romances won't touch. I know; I've seen those people snub the romances on the dollar cart.

I nearly bought a copy of *All Quiet on the Western Front.* An old paperback with some kid's name inked on the flyleaf: Duane R. Templeton. Flipping through, I could see that Duane had stopped underlining passages after page 50 or so. That's about how far I remember getting, back when we'd been assigned *All Quiet on the Western Front* in high school. I didn't finish many of the assigned books in high school.

My wife and I had been arguing about me getting a job. That's what sent me off to the library, along with Joshua, who got this terrible cold the day after Chessie disappeared, an awful, wrenching cold that made him cough deep wet coughs and left him in a sweat on the family room sofa. We let him camp out on the sofa. He liked to watch videos there, neglecting the tall glass of orange juice I'd left for him. I always wanted him to drink more orange juice, because of the cold. But he only took tiny sips every now and then. Mostly he wouldn't even touch the glass.

My high school English teacher was named Mr. Whitney. Mr. Whitney was the one who assigned *All Quiet on the Western Front*. I remember him passing around copies to us—the same paperback edition I found on the dollar cart—while telling us about the book, about the First World War. Mr. Whitney got pretty worked up about it, walking the front of the classroom with a wooden pointer he liked to carry around, sometimes crouching like a batter awaiting a pitch or a golfer lining up a long drive. "Can you imagine," he said, "what it would be like to go off to war tomorrow?" Mr. Whitney paused with the stick held behind his back. "What would that even mean to you?"

My wife and I always argued about me getting a job. I've worked plenty in my life, but never anything steady. Construction, retail, landscaping, food service, that sort of thing. I know I've never been ambitious, but I've always managed to get by. That's what I'd been trying to explain to her when I lost my last job, but she felt doubtful, she said.

"Doubtful," I said. "About what?"

She didn't answer, but I knew what she'd say. *About you.* That's what she'd say, and then I'd ask why, but she wouldn't say anything. She'd just go back to watching TV or reading a magazine without even looking at me. If Joshua were home, they'd play a board game together or make banana bread. Chessie would follow, watching my wife use the mixer. Chessie always got excited about the mixer. He'd crouch himself down on the countertop, something I told my wife I wish she wouldn't allow, and watch the mixer do its thing. Joshua would pet him.

I read the opening page of *All Quiet on the Western Front,* just to have something to do. Normally I wouldn't do that kind of thing, read a book in public, but I was trying to kill time and remember Mr. Whitney and forget about my son and Chessie and the orange juice and the argument with my wife. The opening page was pretty good. *All Quiet on the Western Front* is one of those books that pulls you in on the first page. The first page makes you feel like you're going to finish this book, even when you know you probably won't. That must be why they assign *All Quiet on the Western Front* in so many high schools.

Doubtful. Who doesn't feel doubtful about something at least every once in a while?

I still don't know how I'd answer Mr. Whitney's question. I have no idea how I'd feel about going off to war, besides the obvious. Scared. Terrified. I remember Mr. Whitney walking the room with the stick behind his back, looking at us, daring us to answer. But it's not the kind of question you can answer, really. We just watched him as he paced back and forth. Eventually he sat down on the edge of his desk and spun the stick in his hands. Mr. Whitney had remarkably small hands. People used to make fun.

I carried Duane R. Templeton's copy of *All Quiet on the Western Front* inside the library. I was planning on buying it, but then I started searching online and that took something out of me somehow. It's the loneliest thing, looking for work online. At least with a newspaper you can circle things. *There,* you think, making your little mark. *Maybe.* But searching online feels hopeless. I ended up going to Yahoo! Sports. I always end up going to Yahoo! Sports. I placed Duane R. Templeton's copy of *All Quiet on the Western Front* next to the computer and read box scores, scouting reports.

I had done something before I left the house, something I'd rather not admit. It was when I brought Joshua his third glass of orange juice. He was sitting on the couch the way he'd been doing ever since Chessie disappeared, just watching TV in this absent sort of way, the way everyone looks when they feel lousy and can't do much besides stare at TV. I knew that, but I couldn't help feeling angry at Joshua anyway. Like it was his fault he was so sick. It was the strangest feeling. I set the orange juice beside him and asked him if he wanted to try a little. He shook his head.

"Come on," I said, "try trying." I raised the glass to Joshua's lips. He gave me a surprised look. "Try trying," I repeated, and then I pushed the glass to his lips and tipped it back. But I tipped it so far back that juice spilled over the sides of his mouth. I let it spill. "Try trying," I said again. Joshua looked at me like I was someone he no longer knew. His eyes were wide. When my wife came into the room and asked me why our son was crying, I said I didn't know. Later the two of them sat on the family room floor and drew MISSING CAT posters together. In the posters, Chessie looked sort of happy, pleased. Like he'd escaped. Joshua drew the eyes; my wife added the whiskers. I watched them do that for a while, then left for the library.

For a few weeks after I'd been laid off from the paper mill it was my job to fix Joshua's dinner. That's when my wife was working crazy hours, taking on a part-time job answering phones for QVC. I told her I didn't want her taking a second job, but secretly I was glad: we needed the money. She'd come home from her day job and change into jeans and a sweatshirt, which always made me sort of sad. There's something sad about sweatshirts, but I don't know what it is. She always wore the same one, from a trip we took to Plymouth, Massachusetts, back when taking a trip to Plymouth, Massachusetts, was something we might do. Nowadays we're lucky if we get to the beach once in the summer, the way things cost. Last time we went to the beach, I lost my keys in the ocean and got a forty-dollar parking ticket for parking at a broken meter and it's like what can you do?

The only thing Joshua will eat for dinner is cheese. Cheese and maybe some of the macaroni that's stuck to it, but not much else. Forget about a salad or a vegetable or those little tubs of applesauce my wife keeps buying even though I've never seen Joshua do anything more than lick the lid. Joshua doesn't even like french fries. What kind of kid doesn't like french fries? When I was kid all I'd eat was french fries. The way they'd taste right out of the oven, twirled in ketchup, and you've got something really good on TV. I've always liked eating in front of the TV, even though everyone says eating in front of the TV is terrible, that you should gather round the table like the families in Norman Rockwell paintings, but I'll take my dinner in front of the TV any day, thank you. Makes you feel like you've got company.

So I'd make Joshua his cheese dinner, but Joshua wouldn't eat it. Instead, he'd put his head to the table and start to fall asleep. Other times he'd leave the table and hide. "Joshua?" I'd say, looking for him. "It's time to eat your dinner, buddy." I always hate the way my voice sounds when I'm talking to my kid, like I'm calling a pet out of the rain. Honestly, I wouldn't answer me either. "Joshua? Just eat three more bites and you can have dessert, OK? Come on out, J-man."

Joshua is very good at hiding. Very. He'll hide in places you wouldn't even realize are hiding places. You can forget all about the closet or under the bed or behind the shower curtain—Joshua can fit into the cabinets beneath our end tables, the ones with the smoked-glass doors, which Joshua can pull shut from inside, his body a dark shadow behind the glass. Joshua can slide beneath the guest room comforter without even raising it above the level of the pillows. Walk by and you'll think the bed's just been made. Joshua can wedge himself into the space between the toilet and the bathroom wall, an idea so terrible the one time I found him there I let him go. I was calling out to him, saying, "Come on, Joshua," and Joshua was calling out to me, saying, "I'm right here," in that teeny-tiny Joshua voice of his, even when I was standing in the bathroom looking beneath the sink (no) and sliding the shower curtain back (no again).

"Where are you?" I said.

"I'm right here," he said, and then I saw him there, behind the toilet. He had his head tucked down; his hands clasped together, shoulders at the level of the toilet seat.

"Where are you?" I said again, pretending I hadn't seen him.

"Right here," he said.

"In the hallway?" I said in my voice-that-I-hate voice.

"Right here," Joshua said.

"In the guest room? I bet Joshua's in the guest room."

I turned the bathroom light off and pretended to leave, thinking Joshua would look up to see me go. But he didn't. He just stayed in his hiding spot as I stood in the doorway and waited for him to give up. He made his breaths small and quiet. He kept still. After a while, I walked away and went back to the kitchen and rinsed his dinner plate in the sink.

One time I pulled Joshua's napkin out of his lunchbox without even reading it. I stuffed it into my pocket like it was a gas receipt. I didn't find it until later, when I was sitting around at work, bored, wishing I were someplace else. *Think of me and I'll know,* the note read. I read it again. Then I read it a third time, a fourth. The words seemed out of order somehow, but in perfect order, too. I could read them one way and have the note make sense and read them the other way and feel the hairs on my arms begin to rise. Think of me and I'll know—what? *That you're thinking of me,* of course. But it seemed like the note could mean something else, too. Think of me and I'll know what to do. Or: think of me and I'll know who I am. I wanted to throw the note away, but couldn't. I ended up hiding it inside my desk drawer, back behind the memo pads I could never remember to use. Sometimes I'd open the desk drawer wide enough to see the napkin, when no one was looking. But I never read the note again. I'd close the drawer just as suddenly as I'd opened it.

* * *

After she read Ian's note—the one she knew was coming—my wife went looking for Ian. "I didn't know what else to do," she told me. "I didn't want to tell anyone what had happened. I didn't want to call anyone, didn't want to tell my story, didn't want to cry, not just yet anyway. But I wasn't really angry, either, even though I would be later. Later on I'd call Ian every name in the book, you know. I'd tell all my friends about Ian leaving me on our honeymoon. I'd make it into a funny little story. I'd say how we were young and stupid, it was no one's fault, Ian was still a great guy, I wished him all the best, but really I didn't wish him all the best and it was more his fault than mine. It's funny, but it just felt great to tell people that I still thought Ian was a good guy, despite what he'd done. It was one of the best feelings I've ever had. My husband left me on our honeymoon—but he's super!"

"Magnanimous," I volunteered.

"I guess," my wife said. Then she told me how she went looking for Ian. "I was the one who drove us down to the beach, and the car was still in the lot, so I knew he couldn't have gone very far. Ian hated public transportation, so I knew the bus was out, but you can't really catch a cab in Virginia Beach, not easily anyway."

"Sandy," I said. "The cab would be."

"So I just walked into the café where we had breakfast at the day before, and I knew that's where Ian had been. I remember thinking, 'OK, he got coffee, decided to walk as far away from our hotel as possible, figured he'd hide out for a while until I read the note. That's where he is, hiding out somewhere.' And then I grabbed my coffee and walked outside, realized that's what Ian had done, too, noticed it was already too hot outside, just like Ian had, and decided to walk down the street where we'd been a few days ago, the one with more trees and shade, something Ian had pointed out, how much cooler it was, and I walked in the shade and knew that's where Ian had walked. And I remember thinking how easy this was to figure out. I never had the slightest doubt that I was right on Ian's trail. I remember walking down the street with the knowledge that I was about to see him at any moment. It wasn't even a feeling; I was certain. *You better get ready,* I remember thinking. *Figure out what you're going to say when you see him. That'll be soon.* I walked past all the shops and stores Ian had walked past, knowing I was about to see him and say whatever it was I was going to end up saying to him, and that's when I knew that I really didn't want to find Ian at all. So I turned around and went back to the hotel, dragged our suitcases to the car, and drove home. That was it. I remember pulling into our parking lot and opening the door to our apartment and still feeling like I'd better figure out what I was going to say to Ian, even though I knew Ian wasn't inside the apartment. He was still at the beach, hiding out. I knew that, but I couldn't shake the feeling that I'd better figure out what I'd say to him, and then I remember wishing I'd never see him again, so I wouldn't have to figure out what to say to him. And it wasn't anything like being angry with him, like I would be later on, it was just this weird, total fear of having to figure out what to say to Ian. Because I had no idea what I would say to Ian, and I knew I'd never be able to figure out what to say to him, ever. And that's when I opened the apartment door and saw Ian sitting at our kitchen table, waiting for me. He'd been waiting for me this whole time. He hadn't walked down the shady street. I wasn't right behind him after all. 'How did you get here?' I said, and Ian said, 'I took the bus.' He took the bus. Ian took the bus!"

The day I got home from the library, I saw Chessie sitting at the end of the driveway. He'd perched himself on top of the woodpile I'd let grow over with weeds, licking his paws the way he always did. Already I'd forgotten how he always did that. His fur was matted with dirt, but otherwise he looked the same. He gave me a look when he saw me close the car door. *Don't even,* the look seemed to say.

"Chess-ie," I sang. "He-re, Chessie." I crouched down to the driveway and pretended to offer him a treat. Sometimes that worked for Joshua. But Chessie only went back to licking his paws.

I wanted to call out to Joshua and my wife, Come outside! I found Chessie! He's right here! but I didn't. Instead I walked toward the woodpile, calling out Chessie's name. When I got nearly close enough to grab him, Chessie jumped down from the woodpile and gave me another look.

"Chessie," I said, "it's me."

Chessie blinked his cheerless eyes.

"Where have you been?" I said. "We were all worried."

Chessie began to chew a long piece of grass I really should have gotten with the mower. Maybe he was recalling the times he'd watched me from the sliding glass doors as I mowed the yard. Or maybe he was thinking about all those endless afternoons when we sat watching TV together, me out of work, Chessie stretched out in front of the sliding glass doors, keeping his distance. Could he tell I sometimes thought of opening the doors, wishing him gone?

"Chessie," I said. "Come here."

Chessie backed away. In a moment, I knew, he'd run.

"Chessie."

And then it was on. I grabbed a branch I'd been meaning to break into smaller pieces since forever and chased Chessie across the backyard. He was faster than I expected, ducking under the swing set Joshua hasn't cared about in years, and heading off to the woods that border our yard. I chased him for a good while. I could feel my breath heaving in my chest. I got close enough to see briars clinging to the undersides of his fur. He had nearly reached the woods when I realized I was shouting at him and swinging the stick. *Come out,* I was shouting. *I see you.*